PATTY REED'S DOLL

The Story of the Donner Party

by

Rachel K. Laurgaard

Illustrated by Elizabeth Sykes Michaels
Cover design by Diane Wilde

Tomato Enterprises
PO Box 73892
Davis CA 95617-3892
(530) 750-1832

Copyright 1956 by Caxton Printers, Ltd.
Renewed 1984, Rachel Kelley Laurgaard
Tomato Enterprises Edition, 1989

ISBN 0-9617357-2-4

Library of Congress Catalog Card Number
89-51264

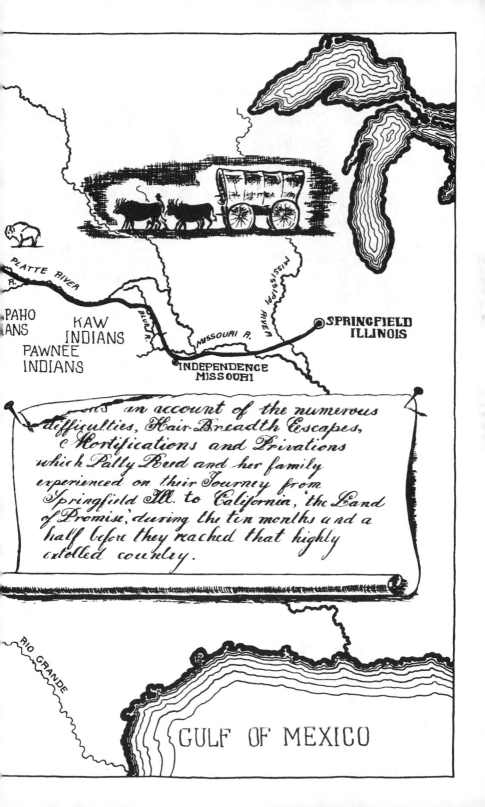

PLATTE RIVER

R.

PAHO
IANS

KAW
INDIANS

PAWNEE
INDIANS

BLUE R.

MISSOURI R.

MISSISSIPPI RIVER

SPRINGFIELD
ILLINOIS

INDEPENDENCE
MISSOURI

... an account of the numerous difficulties, Hair-Breadth Escapes, Mortifications and Privations which Patty Reed and her family experienced on their Journey from Springfield Ill. to California, 'the Land of Promise', during the ten months and a half before they reached that highly extolled country.

RIO GRANDE

GULF OF MEXICO

Patty Reed's doll is now displayed at Sutter's Fort in Sacramento, California. (Photo by Nikki Pahl.)

TABLE OF CONTENTS

LIST OF ILLUSTRATIONS

CHAPTER I

SPRINGFIELD, ILLINOIS, 1846

I AM A little wooden doll with a painted face and a knob of painted hair on top of my wooden head. My cheeks are not so rosy as they once were, nor is my hair so glossy black. But is it any wonder? I was a pioneer, and the trials I have been through would change the face of almost any doll.

I remember well when first I heard of pioneering and covered wagons, Indians and wilderness trails. It was in Grandma's big bedroom back in Springfield, Illinois, on the long winter evenings of 1845. We sat in our rocking chairs—Puss and Patty and I—toasting our toes by the warm fire in the grate and coaxing Grandma to tell us her stories.

Grandma sat, propped up with flouncy pillows, in her high four-poster bed, a knitted shawl around her shoulders and her thin, gray curls tucked into a white nightcap. She was ailing and frail, for she was very old, but her talk was as lively as ever as she told the tales we loved to hear about her childhood in Kentucky.

For Grandma had been a pioneer. She had traveled with her folks over the Wilderness Trail—"Boone's Path" she called it—following the blazed trees that Daniel Boone himself had marked along the narrow, rocky road across the Cumberland Mountains from Virginia to the canebrakes of Kentucky.

All sorts of things she told us about pioneering. "There were creeks to cross with ugly, steep banks," she said. "Our hands were blistered from clinging to the tree roots and vines as we clambered up the slopes, and our legs were scratched by briers and thornbushes. The trail zigzagged up the mountains along narrow ledges, and we could look down through the blue haze and see the green valleys far below. This made us eager to go ahead, for one of those green valleys was to be our new home.

"At night we heard the scary cries of wild animals, and always we were on the lookout for the painted faces of Indians peering through the brush. They would creep like bears through the long grass. All of a sudden, arrows would rain from nowhere, but before we could catch sight of the redskins, they had melted into the woods again. We kept right close to the wagons, I can tell you. We didn't fancy the notion of our scalps being tied to some wild Indian's belt.

"At last, sunburned and leg-weary, we came to the valley where the settlements were. It looked mighty pretty to us, with the trees leafing out and the wind smelling sweet with wild apple blossoms.

"Father and the other men took up claims and commenced to clear the land. They worked from sunup to sundown, chopping trees and grubbing out shrubs and bushes so the corn could be planted before summer. Men were hardy in those days, my dears. Their arms were strong and their axes sharp."

Grandma lay back on her pillows and her dark eyes had a faraway look in them, as though she were back in Kentucky helping her father seed the corn in the fresh-plowed furrows of their new clearing.

Patty and Puss eagerly begged for more, and Grandma went on to tell of fearsome Indian fights and escapes, of how one of their neighbors was killed while searching for his plough horse after it had strayed into the woods, and how her aunt had been spirited away while she was gathering wild strawberries and kept as a slave for five long years in the Indian village away to the north.

As Grandma related this story, Patty's black eyes grew bigger and blacker than ever. She gripped me tightly in her hand, and kept peeping over her shoulder as though the eerie shadows cast by the

flames were really lurking savages ready to pounce
upon us. By the time Grandma had finished her tale,
we were almost too scared to scamper off to bed.
Once there, Patty cuddled me close under the covers,
whispering to me not to be afraid, for she would keep
me safe from Indians. But I think she was the one
who was frightened the most, and it was I who,
nestling up close, reassured her.

After hearing such stories of pioneers and Indians,
imagine how we felt to be told that *we* were to become pioneers! One morning after breakfast, Patty
came hurrying up to her room and, standing before
the window seat where her family of dolls was sitting,
she breathlessly disclosed the news.

"Papa says we are all going to be pioneers across
the plains to California! It will be a healthier place
for Mother, and lots of other people are going in the
spring with wagons and oxen and everything for
keeping house. Isn't it exciting? And you shall all have
new outfits for the journey and a little hair trunk
to pack your best clothes in. I'll have my name put
on it with nailheads—Patty Reed—and then no wild
Indian would dare to steal it, seeing it belongs to
me." We only hoped the Indians would understand
it that way.

As Patty buzzed away to talk it over with Grandma, I tried to explain to the other dolls just how this
piece of news might affect us, for I knew what
pioneering was from having heard Grandma's stories.

They were not too pleased at the prospect. Rosalee
opened her blue eyes wide and complained, "Oh, dear,

I remember well when first I heard of pioneering and covered wagons . . .

I don't believe I shall like being a pioneer doll. My new velvet cloak and sprigged muslin gown may get mudstained and dusty. How dreadful to think of leaving this nice clean window seat to travel in a wagon!"

Minnie, the big wooden doll who was inclined to be of a jealous nature and was always snubbing me because I was only four inches tall, remarked acidly, "Pioneering may be fine for you. You're used to being knocked about. After all, you are just the little country cousin."

She had heard Patty herself make that last remark. But I knew Patty didn't mean it the way Minnie thought she did. Patty loved me best of all her dolls, and she said I was their little country cousin only because my clothes were not so fine as theirs. Patty herself made them for me, while Grandma sewed their elegant outfits.

Patty could not manage her needle quite well enough to do the fine sewing that Grandma did; so, while their dresses had beautiful tucks and ruffles and fine featherstitching, my dress was usually a little square with a hole for my head, sewed together with a few awkward stitches and tied round the middle with a bit of a ribbon sash. But I did not envy my sister dolls their elegance. The gentle touch of Patty's fingers as she carefully bent my wooden joints and pulled the new frock over my painted head, and then proudly held me up for Grandma to see, made me very happy because I was her "little friend." Besides, she spent more time with me than with the others. I was just the right size to ride around in her apron pocket, and thus I came to know much more than they about family doings, and Patty and I shared a secret world all our own.

If Patty was going pioneering, I wanted to go, too. And I guessed the others would feel the same way if it came to a choice between riding in a wagon or being left on some dark closet shelf, as Puss's dolls were. She was fourteen and had forgotten her doll family for a long time now. She had a pony named Billy, and we used to look down from our window seat into the yard below and see her ride out the gate with her father. We wondered if the time would come when we, too, would be gathering dust on the closet shelf while Patty rode out with the grownups.

But that time had not yet come. Patty was only eight and, so far, she would rather sit and sew at Grandma's bedside, run with messages downstairs to her mother or Eliza in the kitchen, or play with her little brothers, Tommy and Jimmy—always with me in her apron pocket. Yes, if there was any dust to be gathered, I much preferred to gather it out on the trail with Patty than on a shelf in a dark closet.

I was present in Patty's apron pocket when the family gathered around Grandma's bed that afternoon to talk over the pioneering venture with her. Mr. and Mrs. Reed, Patty's father and mother, plainly did not think that Grandma would be able to go with them, and they gently tried to explain how Uncle Gershom, Grandma's eldest son, and his wife would come to live in the big white house that we should be leaving, and that Grandma would stay right where she was in her comfortable bed, and they would take good care of her.

The old lady sat up bright and sudden at the thought of this. "Now you listen here, James Frazier Reed," I heard her say, "You're not taking daughter Margaret and these grandchildren of mine one step of the way West unless I go along. I guess I know a heap more about pioneering than you do, and I'm not a-fixin' to be left behind!"

Well, they did a bit more pleading with her but in the end she got her way, and I must say that I for one was glad to know that we were to have so experienced a pioneer as Grandma with us on our dangerous journey through the Indian country.

During the next few weeks I kept my ears open to pick up bits of information to relay to my sister dolls who were gradually becoming reconciled to the thought of the journey. I told them I had heard Mrs. Reed say that there were others from Springfield going West in April—two families by the name of Donner, friends of the Reeds, who had several children Patty's and Puss's age and some little ones like Tommy and Jimmy. In their Saturday night reading club they had been reading a book about California by a Mr. Hastings, who said that there was so much sunshine that chills and fever and aching bones were unknown. The land was rich and good for several crops a year, and the Americans who were settled out there said there was room for many more.

The mothers did not think much of the idea at

first, but as the cold Illinois winter dragged on, and
Patty's mother had so many headaches and miseries,
she was at last persuaded that life would be much
better in California, and once she made up her mind
to go, the Donner mothers decided to go, too.

It wasn't long after the winter snows melted that
activities began in the yard below. While Grandma
and Mrs. Reed did great quantities of sewing indoors,
preparations of a different sort were going on outside. We dolls, looking down from our seat at the
upstairs window, judged that it must be a very long
way to California by the amount of activity we saw.

One day two enormous wagons were drawn into
the yard. Box after box of food was stowed away in
them by Milt Elliott and Bayless Williams, the two
hired men who were going with us. Big, good-
natured Eliza Williams, our cook, was Bayless's sister,
and she was going, too. Other men were going to
help drive the oxen and take care of the cattle. They
were all down in the yard below us packing the
wagons and shouting remarks at one another.

Mr. Reed stood by checking things off on his long
list as they were hoisted into the wagon: barrels of
flour, corn meal, and sugar; rice, beans, peas, crackers,
dried fruit, preserves, honey, vinegar, salt; hams, beef,
and smoked fish. We dolls had no idea that people
required so much food.

Then there were other lists for Patty's father to
check. Tools of all sorts—axes, hatchets, sickles ("to
cut grass on long drives," I heard him say to Milt)
spades, saws, nails, whetstones, tacks, needles, pins,

thread, scissors, wax, sail needles, twine, hammers, rope, chains; beeswax and tallow melted together for greasing shoes; rosin and tallow for wheels; guns and bullet molds and bars of lead to make the bullets. ("Oh, dear," we recalled, "that's in case of Indian attacks!")

From time to time other men who, we gathered, were taking their families to California, stopped by to see how the Reeds were coming along.

"You'd better plan to sell some of your horses and buy oxen," we heard Mr. Reed tell one of them. "Horses are likely to stall in mudholes, you know, and oxen can live off the grass on the way. Packing feed for the horses will take up too much of your wagon space."

"Hadn't thought of it in that way," the man said. "Guess you're right, Mr. Reed."

One morning another, stranger looking wagon was drawn up in the yard. This must be the one we had heard the family refer to as the "Palace Car." Mr. Reed was having it built especially comfortable for Grandma.

"It's to be our home on wheels," Patty told us. "See, the door is on the side instead of at the end like the other wagons. And there are spring seats inside and a little iron stove to keep us warm. There's the stovepipe going up through the top, with a piece of tin around it to keep the sparks from falling on the canvas wagon top. And just look! It has two stories! Isn't that funny—a wagon with an upstairs, and beds? A regular traveling house!"

Bedding and cooking utensils and clothes, in big canvas sacks, were put into the Palace Car. The Reeds didn't take any trunks. "They are useless weight," Patty's father said. But we dolls had our little hair trunk, as Patty promised; and, although it contained mainly the fashionable gowns of my sister dolls, I, too, had a few scraps tucked away in it, from which Patty had promised to make a new dress as we traveled.

At last the day came for departure. It was the fourteenth of April, 1846, as I have heard Patty relate many times since then. The birds were singing in the lilac bushes outside our window, and spring flowers were blossoming in the yard of the big white house that we were leaving forever. Patty and Puss were dressed in their new linsey traveling suits, and I was safely cradled in Patty's pocket. Mr. Reed was dignified and handsome in black broadcloth, and Mrs. Reed was wearing her best Paisley shawl and Sunday bonnet.

The men led teams of oxen into the yard and yoked them to the wagons. Mr. Reed's mare Glaucus was pawing the ground, and Puss's pony Billy was prancing around as excited as his mistress. Relatives and neighbors were gathered to bid the Reeds good-by.

"Here, Margaret," we heard one lady say to Mrs. Reed, "I've brought you a looking glass. Hang it where you can take a peep at yourself now and then, so you won't forget to keep your good looks." Patty's mother laughingly thanked her and hung it opposite the door in the Palace Car.

Soon there was great barking of dogs and shouting as more wagons rolled up the road. Some one called out, "Here are the Donners." Patty was arranging us in the Palace Car by this time, and several other little girls popped their heads in to see what was going on.

"Oh, are you allowed to take all your dolls?" one of them asked Patty. "We could only take our best ones. We had to give the old ones away."

I heard this remark with dismay. "Dear me," I thought, "is it possible Patty might have to leave me behind?" But I was soon reassured as she answered, "We have plenty of room for everything, and I wouldn't give any of my dolls away for anything." Her little hand closed around me and made me feel warm and secure.

Never had we been in the midst of so many laughing and chattering and crying people. All of Patty's and Puss's schoolmates were there to kiss them good-by.

"What luck, kids!" one little boy remarked, "I wish my folks were going to California."

Uncle James and Uncle Gershom still tried to persuade Grandma to change her mind and remain with them, as they lifted her onto her feather bed in the Palace Car. But Grandma was as determined as ever to "go a-pioneerin'" once again.

At last the drivers, one by one, cracked their whips and the oxen moved the wagons slowly out onto the road.

Patty sat on Grandma's bed, holding up the wagon flap so we could all have one last look at our old home and the cheering, waving friends we were leaving behind.

Through the streets of Springfield, Milt Elliott drove the Palace Car. "Milt," I heard Puss call as she rode by on Billy, "are you sure you can get the oxen to keep the wagon on that narrow bridge? Without reins, how can you make them go where you want them to?"

Milt laughed and called back, "Don't you worry, Puss. Bully and George are the best pair of lead oxen in the party. They know what 'whoa' and 'haw' and 'gee' mean as well as I do."

Several of the family dogs were going with us, and they pranced proudly alongside the wagons, paying not the least attention as curious Springfield dogs came up to bark and sniff as we rolled by.

"Are you comfortable, Grandma?" asked Patty.

"Fine, child, fine," answered the old lady, her eyes sparkling. I suppose she was remembering when she was Patty's age and starting on that other trek down the Wilderness Road, the one which she had told us of so often.

Jimmy and Tommy busied themselves inspecting the cupboards under the seats, pulling at the knobs and squatting down to peer into them inquisitively, and repeating a hundred times, "What's this, Mommy? What's this?"

"We won't travel far today, Mother," Mrs. Reed said to Grandma. "The men intend to set up camp just as they will when we get out on the plains. Besides, Jim and Gershom and some of the Donners friends plan to ride out and camp with us for a farewell party tonight."

"Yes, they don't like the idea of their old mother a-goin' pioneering at her age. But you know I'll be happier with you, dear, as long as I last. . . . How many of us are there, Daughter?"

"Thirty-one, I believe Mr. Reed said. A good number for three families. The Donners are fine folks, quiet and sensible. They have some nice youngsters, too. Ours won't lack playmates. . . . Mrs. George Donner plans to start a school in California."

"With fourteen young ones in the party, it will be a lively crossing, I reckon," Grandma said.

CHAPTER II

THE FIRST NIGHT OUT

WE HADN'T been long out of Springfield when the order to halt was called down the line. As soon as the Palace Car came to a stop, Patty, with me in her pocket, jumped out to watch the first camp making. The Donner children came tumbling out of their wagons and, with the dogs barking, the children shouting, and the cattle mooing and milling around, it's a wonder the men were able to get any order at all.

They finally got the wagons arranged in a large circle in the grassy field where we had halted. The tongue of each wagon was drawn up close to the tailboard of the wagon ahead of it. Then the oxen were unyoked and led out to graze on the tender spring grass where the cows were already munching. Tents for the men to sleep in were pitched inside the circle. The women and children slept in the wagons.

Back in the Palace Car, Eliza and Mrs. Reed were already fixing dinner just as though they were back home in their kitchen in Springfield. A little cookstove had been set up, and the smell of meat cooking and biscuits baking soon drew the children back to their home wagons.

After dinner, we heard the thump of hoofs on the dirt road, and more people from Springfield arrived. Uncle James and Uncle Gershom looked in to see how Grandma had liked her first day's journey.

"It's as cozy a bedroom as a body could want," she told them. "They still think I'll give up and turn back with them," she whispered to Patty after the two men had left to help with the bonfire that was being built outside.

The editor of the Springfield paper was there talking to Mr. and Mrs. Reed about the condition of the roads through Illinois.

"You must send back a full account of everything. There'll be plenty of folks hereabouts who'll be anxious to follow you out next spring. Sort of wish I were going myself," he said. And Mr. Reed promised to send back word by any they should meet who were returning.

Everyone gathered around the high, roaring bonfire, laughing and singing and telling stories, mostly

Patty, with me in her pocket, jumped out to watch the first camp making

about that wonderful land we were going to—California, where people were healthy and happy, and flowers bloomed all the year round.

Soon the youngest children were led back to the wagons and tucked into bed. Patty and twelve-year-old Leanna Donner, and the two fourteen-year-olds, Puss and Elitha Donner, were allowed to stay up and sing songs with the grownups. But it had been a day full of excitement, and it wasn't long before Patty was yawning, and her mother, catching sight of her sleepy little daughter, motioned to her that it was bedtime.

Grandma was still awake when Patty climbed back into the wagon, and she whispered to her as she undressed, "Do you think they can see our bonfire back in Springfield, Grandma?"

"I wouldn't doubt, child, that there's many back there who are watching tonight and wishing us luck," the old lady said.

CHAPTER III

FROM SPRINGFIELD TO INDEPENDENCE

NEXT MORNING the lowing of the cattle and the shouts of the men woke the children at sunrise. Eliza in her calico apron was already getting breakfast, and the smell of bacon and johnnycake made them hurry to dress and be out in the fresh April daylight.

"Patty, dear, take your little brothers out and wash their faces." Mrs. Reed was buttoning the little boys' shoes as they wriggled around among the quilts.

"All right, Mother." Patty tied her apron strings and slipped me out from under her pillow and into her pocket.

With the children's faces scrubbed and shining (the washbasin sat on the tailboard of one of the other wagons), and their hair all neatly combed, the family was ready for breakfast. Puss and her father had returned from feeding the horses, and the men from their morning chores.

Patty took Grandma's breakfast in to her first, and then sat down on a campstool outside to eat her own. The grass was still wet with dew, and I noticed everyone shivered now and then in the crisp morning air.

When the dishes had been washed and packed away and the patchwork quilts spread neatly over the beds, Patty asked if we could sit up on the box with Milt for "a ways." Her mother gave her permission, and Milt boosted us up over the high front wheels to the seat beside him.

From this perch we looked down the line on last-minute preparations. Men were rounding up the cattle and women were rounding up the children. Grease was being put on the wheel hubs, and oxen were being yoked. The big animals, frisky after their night's rest, tossed their heads and clanked their chains trying to throw off the heavy yokes. It wasn't long before they were ready, the drivers on their boxes with whips in hand, the women and children in the wagons, and Puss and Mr. Reed at the head of the line on Glaucus and Billy.

"Catch up! Catch up!" the order rang out, and wagons began to roll.

Day after day for almost a month we plodded

Day after day for almost a month we plodded down the muddy roads of Illinois . . .

down the muddy roads of Illinois, past farmhouses where dogs ran out to bark and people waved to us as we rode by. Cherry and crab-apple and wild plum blossoms reminded Grandma of Kentucky springs, and there were strawberry runners and winding grape vines in the fields where we camped at night. The wagon tops stayed white in the blue, rainwashed April air, but underfoot the mud was thick and sticky.

Grandma said she felt better every day. "A good case of Western fever was just what these old bones needed," she told Patty.

"What's 'Western fever,' Grandma?" I was glad Patty asked, because I was wondering, too, how one sickness could help her get well from another one.

"Well, child, it's a powerful urge to go a-pioneering, that's what it is. And now that I'm doing just that, I am better already."

Grandma certainly was as pert as ever. With her piece bag always at hand, she kept her fingers busy piecing quilt blocks, while Patty sat beside her making a dress for me. I thanked my lucky stars that I was just "the little country cousin" and could "knock about" with Patty. The other dolls were carefully packed away in the cupboard under the seats, lest their fragile faces and beautiful dresses should be damaged by the roughness of the trip, while here I was, out in full view of the world and able to take in everything.

When it rained and things were dull for Tommy and Jimmy, we all played hide-the-thimble. The

Palace Car was too small to really hide it, so we just pretended, and then the others guessed. That way Grandma could play too, without ever getting up from bed.

Sometimes Patty took me over to the Donner wagons, and all the little girls played with their dolls. Mrs. Donner was an artist, and she let us look at her sketch book where she had pressed the flowers we found along the way and had drawn pretty pictures of them. She told us that's what it meant to "botanize."

On dry nights we had a campfire and sat around it visiting until bedtime. Mr. Reed wrote down the record of each day's progress in a little book he kept in his vest pocket and, from that, he could tell how far we were along the way.

It was the evening of May 10, as I remember, that he told us, "Tomorrow we'll be camping at the outskirts of Independence."

"Independence is the last town on the frontier, isn't it, Papa?" asked Puss.

"Yes, and I've been thinking I'd see about arranging for two or three more wagonloads of provisions when we get there. It will be better to have too much than too little when we are out on the prairie. California is a mighty long ways away!"

"I'd like to buy some sunbonnets for the girls and myself, if we have a chance. The ones we brought won't be much protection, I'm afraid," said Mrs. Reed.

The clouds of small buzzing wings that hovered

over us soon drove all the folks back to the wagons for the night.

"Dolly, you are lucky that your face is made of wood, and the pesky skeeters can't bite you," said Patty, as the hand that held me came up with a jerk to drive one of the whirring insects away from her ear.

CHAPTER IV

INDEPENDENCE, MISSOURI

NEXT MORNING, after a short drive, we reached the outskirts of Independence and made our encampment. Patty and I stayed with Grandma and the boys while Mr. and Mrs. Reed and Puss rode into town.

After a while Puss and her mother came back and unwrapped the bundles to show us what they had bought.

"How do I look in my new sunbonnet, Mother?" asked Mrs. Reed, as she tried on a yellow straw-braid bonnet in front of her little mirror.

"Fine, Daughter," answered Grandma. "That should keep the freckles off your nose, and shade your eyes from the Western sun."

"Grandma, see my new parasol," grinned Puss. "We brought one for you, too, Patty."

"Mercy, child, can you carry a parasol and hold Billy's reins at the same time?"

"Of course, Grandma. I need only one hand for Billy's reins."

"Where's Papa?" Patty asked.

"We left him in front of the wagonworks bargaining with a noisy outfitter for some more wagons and supplies," her mother answered.

"And guess what, Patty? We saw some Indians! They weren't like Grandma's Indians, though. These didn't have feathers in their hair, or bows and arrows. They were just dark-skinned men in ragged, dirty clothes—some of them with rings in their ears." Puss knew this would be exciting news.

"They were Mexican and Indian traders," Mrs. Reed explained, "Just in from Santa Fe. Independence is where they come to get outfitted."

"They had poor, tired-looking mules, so skinny their ribs showed, and horses with little bells jingling on their harnesses, and long trains of ox teams pulling queer, tented wagons," Puss continued.

"The Santa Fe Trail is a hard journey over deserts and through mountains. That is why they looked so battered and footsore," Mrs. Reed added.

"Do you suppose we will look that way when we arrive in California?" Patty wondered.

Mr. Reed returned around dinnertime and told us more about the bustling town of Independence.

"I met a Mr. Thornton who is emigrating to Oregon with his invalid wife, and a family by the name

"How do I look in my new sunbonnet, Mother?" asked Mrs. Reed, as she tried on a yellow straw-braid bonnet in front of her little mirror.

of Boggs from Missouri. They are waiting here for
a Mr. Boone and his family from Kentucky."

"Boone?" spoke up Grandma. "Must be some kin of
old Daniel." Her eyes lighted up at the mention
of this familiar pioneer name.

Mr. Reed smiled as he answered, "Yes, ma'am, a
grandson, I was told. When Mr. Boone gets here,
they all plan to hurry on to join Colonel Russell's
California Company. They are waiting out there on
the Kansas River."

"Do you think we could join them, too?" Mrs.
Reed asked. "The more wagons there are in our
train, the safer we'll be when we get to Indian
territory."

Patty squeezed me tighter at the mention of that
dread word, "Indian," and we both leaned over
anxiously to hear Mr. Reed's answer.

"Yes, I have talked it over with George and Jacob
Donner, and they agree that it would be a good plan
to overtake Colonel Russell and apply for admission
to his train. We'd best not dillydally in Independence
any longer than necessary. Folks hereabouts seem
to think that nigh onto seven thousand wagons will
go west this season. The first ones across will have
the best pasturage and water."

Next morning, early, the men yoked up the reluctant oxen and headed in the bellowing cattle, and
we were again on our way. The streets of Independence were as noisy and muddy and crowded as Puss
had said they were. Ox teams, mule teams, and freight
wagons of all sorts blocked the road while their

owners haggled over prices. We stuck out our heads to see the Santa Fe traders we had been told about and, as we rolled by, people waved and called out "Good luck," just as they had back in Springfield. As we turned our backs on the morning sun and headed west, we heard Milt shout, "Good-by, Independence! Ho, for California!"

CHAPTER V

OUT ON THE PRAIRIE

THOSE FIRST days out on the prairie, after crossing the Missouri River, were like one long picnic. The grassy meadows stretched away and away with no sign of house or town or even trees, only blue sky coming down to meet green plains. And, oh, the flowers!

"It's like a big garden, Grandma," said Patty lifting the wagon flap to look out. "May I get down and pick a bouquet, Mother?"

"If you will stay close by, you may. Take the boys with you. They need to stretch their legs a bit," her mother said.

The dogs came bounding up to greet us and followed us into the fields. Frances and Leanna Donner jumped out of their wagon to join us, too; and the three little girls began busily filling their aprons with flowers.

"The pink ones are verbena," Leanna told the other two. "Mother knows the names of all of them. We must take some to her for her scrapbook."

"What are the blue ones that look like bean blossoms?" Patty held up one she had just picked.

"Wild indigo, I think Mother called them. Some of the blue ones are larkspur."

Mrs. Donner lifted four-year-old Georgia and three-year-old Eliza down from the high wagon, and they came running over to trail along behind us with Tommy and Jimmy.

"The bluebells are blue, too, Leanna." Six-year-old Frances knew the names of the flowers her mother had taught them almost as well as did her twelve-year-old sister.

"That's right, Frances. And here are some wild geraniums," Leanna answered.

"My mother says that your mother is going to have a school when we get to California. Maybe I can go to it. Papa is bringing a big box of books, too. He says books will be hard to get in California." Patty imparted this information as she stopped to weave blossoms in Leanna's blonde braids.

"I wonder if I could make a flower garland for Dolly?" Patty took me out of her pocket and tried a bluebell on my head for size.

"Those tiny red flowers that grow close to the

ground would make a cunning wreath for your dolly," Leanna suggested.

We had been having such a good time in those sweet-smelling fields of flowers that we didn't notice that a dark cloud had begun to cover the sun, until Mrs. Reed and Mrs. Donner both called to the children to hurry back before the rain came down.

Soon the sky was completely black and large raindrops had begun to fall. Brilliant streaks of lightning flashed, and thunder followed them.

Puss and her father came galloping back to the wagon. Puss dismounted to ride with us while it rained, and Mr. Reed tied Billy's halter to a stake at the tail of the wagon. Mrs. Reed got out his oilskin coat, and he rode on ahead again. And how it poured, beating hard on the canvas wagon top and running down the sides in great streams!

"I hope it stops before suppertime," Puss remarked. "The evenings are so dreary when we can't have a campfire."

"These prairie thunderstorms do rise up of a sudden," said Grandma. "But then, they let up that quick, too." And she was right. The storm was over soon and out came the sun.

"Oh, look at the rainbow!" Patty exclaimed, raising the wagon flap to see what the wet world outside was like. "It's so clear and bright I can almost reach out and touch it."

> "Red, yellow, and Irish green,
> The King can't touch it,
> No more can the Queen,"

Patty took me out of her pocket and tried a bluebell on my head for size

recited Grandma. "That's what my grandmother used to say when we saw the rainbow curving over the Kentucky hills. And I reckon her grandmother told it to her back in the old country where they had kings and queens."

"And I shall remember to say it when I am a grandma, too," said Patty, as I tried to think of little pink-cheeked Patty grown old and wrinkled like Grandma. In a way, though, I fancied they were quite alike. Grandma's bright black eyes were so like Patty's when they sparkled.

"You shall have many an exciting tale to store up for your grandchildren by the time this jaunt is over," said Grandma.

For about a week the oxen plodded along, sometimes bogging down in the deep, muddy ruts left by the wagons up ahead.

Grandma worked on her patchwork when the going wasn't too rough. Mrs. Reed sat on the comfortable spring seat knitting, while Patty tried to amuse Jimmy and Tommy who were restless on wet days when they couldn't get out and run.

The cows and little calves at the back of the train kept up a constant mooing and bawling. They got tired of being driven along all day. Occasionally the dogs barked at them to keep them from wandering, and sometimes Mr. Reed had to go back to help the men drive them along.

At night, in spite of all they could do to keep them "corraled," as I heard them say, some of the cattle wandered, and Milt and Bayless and the other men had to ride out and round them up before breakfast. If they were tied, they got so tangled in the ropes that they would throw themselves before morning. They weren't enjoying this pioneering adventure as much as we were.

One afternoon, Puss came galloping back to tell us that we were almost to the Kansas River, where we would have to be ferried across.

"Father rode ahead this morning to make arrangements with the ferrymen. I heard him tell Uncle George Donner that they were Indians."

"Indians," exclaimed Grandma, "Mercy! They may scalp us all."

"They must be safe, or Father wouldn't let them take us." Mrs. Reed tried to sound reassuring, but looked apprehensive in spite of herself.

"Oh, they're tame Indians, I guess," Puss said. "Father says they have already carried a large wagon train over ahead of us."

"That must be Colonel Russell's company. Did Father say we'd overtake them today?" Mrs. Reed asked her.

"They are three miles ahead of us, the ferrymen told him, camped on Soldier's Creek. Father thinks we'll come up with them before night."

We had been traveling through thick woods for the last few miles. The underbrush crackled beneath the wagon wheels, and the branches of the trees scraped against the canvas wagon top. Finally we came out close to a boat landing on the bank of the Kansas River.

The men were already driving the cattle into the river to make them swim across, and Milt and Bayless began unyoking the oxen so they could follow. Two ferryboats were moored at the landing, and Mr. Reed and Uncle George and Uncle Jacob Donner were trying to reach an agreement with the Indians about the price. One dollar per wagon they had charged the other party, they said.

We watched with great interest as the men lifted each wagon onto the ferryboats, two wagons on each boat. When our turn came, we sat very still as they hoisted us up in mid-air and set us carefully down in the wobbly boat. Patty held up the wagon flap so we could see what was going on, while her mother held Tommy and Jimmy by her side to keep them from tumbling head first out into the river in their curiosity to see everything, especially the Indians. They were all eyes and full of questions, as usual.

"If they drop us, will we break?" Jimmy asked.

"They won't drop us, dear. They are very strong and careful," his mother said.

"Those men don't look like Indians, Mamma. Where are their feathers?" Jimmy persisted.

"Tame Indians don't wear feathers. Only wild ones do," Patty informed him.

The wheels of our wagon were locked with chains and tied securely to the sides of the boat. It wouldn't do to roll while we were in midstream. The ferrymen pushed the boats across with long poles and, as we watched their strong rhythmical movements, we decided they must be very good Indians to help us like this. Perhaps all the fierce, unfriendly Indians were gone since Grandma was a girl.

While the rest of the wagons were being ferried across, Patty's mother let her and the boys get out and stretch their legs. They found that the banks were covered with wild strawberries and they set about filling the bucket Eliza handed them.

"We'll have strawberries and cream for supper tonight, Dolly," Patty said to me. "Don't you wish you could open your tiny mouth and taste one? See how shiny and red they are." I could not tell her, but I think she knew I lived on love, not mortal food.

CHAPTER VI

COLONEL RUSSELL'S COMPANY

THAT AFTERNOON we came up with Colonel Russell's
company. Patty and I, sitting on the box with Milt,
saw the white-topped wagons in the distance, part
of them with "California" painted on their canvas,
the rest with "Oregon." As we rode closer, we could
see the women washing in the creek and hanging
clothes on the bushes to dry in the bright sunshine.
Some of the men were fishing, while others were
working on their wagons. The children, as Milt said,
were "busy as bird dogs doing nothing."

Patty's father, arriving ahead of us, had dismounted

from his gray mare and was talking to a portly gentleman with a heavy, gold watch chain across his broad chest and a pleasant smile on his face. As Milt brought the oxen to a halt and lifted us down to the ground, Mr. Reed said, "Colonel Russell, this is Mr. Elliott from Springfield, and this is my little daughter, Patty."

Colonel Russell shook hands with Milt and Patty, and said to them both, in a stately way, "I am exceedingly delighted to have the privilege of meeting you."

Then Mr. Reed took him to the door of the Palace Car to meet the other members of the family. We heard the genial Colonel tell Mrs. Reed and Grandma that he and his party would be happy to have such solid citizens as the Donner and Reed families travel in their company.

Patty and I skipped off to see what Leanna and Frances were up to, and to make note of any other little girls who might be Patty's age.

That night we had a roaring bonfire, and around it everyone got acquainted. There was a large jolly family named Breen—all boys, to Patty's disappointment, except for baby Isabella. But Mrs. Breen was a hearty, happy soul who took a shine to Patty and Puss. When she found out that Mr. Reed's folks had come from Ireland, she said to Puss, "I was thinking I saw a bit of Irish sparkle in those dancing eyes. It's good to be seeing a pretty colleen the likes of you about, and me and old Pat with none but boys, excepting the wee one there."

"Old Pat" was her husband, and it wasn't long before he'd won our hearts, too, with his fiddle music. For his wife he played "When First I Saw Sweet Peggy," and a gay young man who was traveling with them, named Pat Dolan, sang the words, while a good many others joined in. After that there was more singing, "Yankee Doodle," "Annie Laurie," "The Girl I Left Behind Me." Some one suggested "Home, Sweet Home," but the rest shouted, "Oh, no! Not that! We mustn't get homesick yet!" Mr. Breen's fiddle broke into the strains of "Old Dan Tucker" and the boys jumped up, grabbing the girls by the hand and starting to dance on the green prairie. Then there was "Skip to My Lou" and "Hey, Betty Martin," and finally Pat Dolan danced an Irish jig on the tailboard of a wagon while the rest all clapped, and the lively music made my tiny blue slippers feel like jigging, too.

The girls told Grandma all about it as they crawled into bed, tired but happy. And Puss said of Patrick Dolan, "He could charm the birds right out of the trees."

Next day we traveled for several miles over a wet, boggy plain between the Kansas River and Soldier's Creek. By three o'clock the rain was pouring down and the men decided it would be best to halt on a high ridge of ground and make camp. There was no bonfire that night, and supper was cooked on the small stove inside the Palace Car.

Patty's father came in to sit with us till bedtime and talk about our plans.

Pat Dolan sang the words, while a good many others joined in

"Some of the folks think we are traveling too slowly," he said. "A party of wagons bound for Oregon is going to leave Colonel Russell's company and move ahead faster." And he added thoughtfully, "Perhaps we'd be wise to join them."

"We have plenty of supplies, James, and it's better not to tire out the oxen at the beginning of the journey, isn't it?" Patty's mother said.

"It isn't that that's worrying me. This is the easy part of the trip. But we must be sure to get past the mountains before there is danger of snowstorms."

"Yes," said Grandma, "I've heard tell of parties who tried to cross the Cumberland Mountains too late in the season and got snowed in for the winter and like to have starved to death. When they wandered down into the settlements in the spring, they were perfect scarecrows of folks." Patty and I, listening to the conversation, shuddered at this horrid thought.

"The Donners and I thought we'd discuss it with Colonel Russell tomorrow. We should be making at least ten miles a day."

The prairies were sweet-smelling after the rain and the meadow larks were singing in the morning sunshine as the wagons lurched and swayed over the wet roads next day.

Puss came back to tell us that we'd be crossing a creek with steep banks before long.

"Father and the other men are exploring the slopes to see if there is any break in them where the wagons can roll down easily. If they can't find a place, they'll have to lower the wagons with ropes."

Tommy and Jimmy were excited at the prospect of another ride through the air, but Grandma told them, "I reckon the men who do the back work don't admire this sort of crossing as much as you young ones do."

With ropes and hooks and various lines they got the wagons down and, after crossing the creek, the ox teams were doubled up to haul us up the opposite bank. It took from noon to four o'clock to complete the job and, by the time our wagon got to the other side, the ones ahead had already made camp on high, dry ground about a mile away.

"Oh, goody, a picnic," exclaimed Jimmy as our wagon came to a halt and he saw white tablecloths spread on the grass. The little Donner boys came whooping out ahead, and before their mothers could think to warn them to keep clean for supper, they had found a mud hole of just the right softness for mud pies.

After dinner the men amused themselves with target practice until dark, while the children played hide-and-seek among the wagons. There was a blazing campfire that night and, while the older folks sat around it visiting, the young ones coaxed Uncle Patrick, as they all called Mr. Breen, to get out his fiddle and rosin up the bow for some music and dancing.

When Mr. Reed looked in at bedtime, he told Grandma that we had come only six miles that day.

At breakfast next morning we had a visitor. No less a personage than an Indian chief came and sat down with us, uninvited. Mr. Reed said "How do you do?" to him, and he answered "How" and helped himself to Eliza's corn bread and bacon.

The children could not help staring round-eyed at our strange guest with his ears and neck hung with trinkets and buttons of bone and tin that jangled each time he moved. He must have noticed we were staring at him, for he leaned over to point out, especially, a medal hanging among the other bangles on his necklace. On one side was a picture of John Tyler, President of the United States, and on the other side a pipe and a tomahawk and the words "Peace and Friendship." Mr. Reed read them to us, and the children and their mother smiled politely to let the Indian know they admired it. After breakfast, Mr. Reed offered him some tobacco, which he accepted without saying "Thank you," and got up and left. Eliza said, "Well, I swan." And she scrubbed the dishes extra hard.

We saw many of his tribesmen that day, for we found we had camped only two miles from a very large Indian village. Kaws, they called themselves, and not all of them were as polite as our breakfast guest. They swarmed around the wagons begging for food and buttons and clothes—in fact, for anything they took a fancy to. Most of them were wrapped in dirty blankets and leggings, and all had ornaments of bone and tin and brass on their ears and necks, and even in their noses. Some of them had red paint on their faces and their hair was tangled and matted.

"Are they like the Kentucky Indians?" Patty asked Grandma.

"Land, child, I never was that close to so many of them afore. But I reckon Indians are Indians wherever you find them, and I hope the men will think to double the guard on the camp tonight."

For several days the Kaw Indians followed us and we began to feel sorry for them. They seemed so hungry and eager to accept anything that was offered them.

"Why don't they hunt and get food that way?" Patty asked her father.

"They do, Patty," he told her, "but the game is being driven farther and farther west by emigrants and trappers, so before long they will have nothing but roots and berries to eat."

That day we passed a party of trappers returning to the settlements. They were packing several large sacks of furs and suspended from their saddles were wild turkeys, raccoons, and squirrels.

CHAPTER VII

ON THE BANKS OF THE BIG BLUE

THE MEADOWS we were traveling through were still beautiful and full of flowers—wild roses, honeysuckle, and tulips. Mrs. Donner went gathering them with the children. She said that as long as there were Indians around she wanted to keep the youngsters in sight. "You never can tell when they might take a notion they'd like to carry a white baby back to their village along with the buttons and beads and food they get from us," she said to Patty's mother. Mrs. Reed agreed with her and was grateful to her for keeping an eye on the Reed children, too, while she was watching over Grandma.

The old lady's cough had taken a turn for the

On the banks of the Big Blue River

worse. "It's the damp weather," Mrs. Reed told Mrs. Donner. "If only we could get into higher, dryer country, I feel sure she would improve. She's far from her old lively self these last few days."

But dear Grandma never got to dryer country. On the evening of May 26 we camped on the banks of the Big Blue River, expecting to cross it next day. But there had been so many rains lately and the stream was so much swollen and rushing with a strong, rapid current—which rose that night until the muddy waters were even with the top of its banks— that we had to remain encamped there for several days while the men set to work to build a ferryboat to get the wagons across.

Grandma's cough continued to get worse. Eliza kept a kettle of tea hot on the little stove in the Palace Car and, all night long, Mrs. Reed sat by her bed ministering to her needs. Peeping out from under Patty's pillow I could see the worried lines on her tired face, and I knew that all was not well with Grandma.

On the third night we had been encamped on the Big Blue, Grandma had a bad spell. Her cough kept the children awake, and Patty and Puss went up into the second story of the wagon where the boys were put to bed to quiet them and tell them stories until they went to sleep. After awhile, Grandma's coughing stopped and the girls, too, dropped off to sleep.

Perhaps poor Grandma will be better now, I thought. And Mrs. Reed can get some rest. Everything was still for a long while. Then I heard quiet sobbing, and Mr. Reed's low voice.

In the morning he came up to tell the children that their dear Grandma had come as far as she was able. We would have to go the rest of the way West without her. They all cried and their father tried to comfort them by saying that the angels had come to take Grandma so she wouldn't suffer any more.

Everything was very quiet in camp that day. The boat building stopped and the carpenters went to work building a coffin from a big cottonwood tree, and that afternoon Grandma was buried in a flowery meadow under an oak tree. The Reverend Mr. Cornwall, who was in the party, read the service, and John Denton, a teamster with the Donner family, who had been a stonecutter, made a marker for her grave.

CHAPTER VIII

THE VALLEY OF THE PLATTE

FOR SEVERAL more days, boat making took up the attention of the men and boys. Tommy and Jimmy, along with the rest, jumped up and down on the bank and cheered as the *Blue River Rover* was christened and launched. She floated like a cork and was put to work immediately, ferrying the wagons across.

From the valley of the Blue we rose out on a high, rolling prairie covered with luxuriant grass. There were fewer trees than before and these were mostly clustered around the small creeks where we camped.

Life went on much as before. Breakfast was the main business in the cold, crisp mornings with the sun slanting from the east. The lowing of the cattle, neighing of the horses, and clucking of the chickens as they laid eggs for breakfast started things up lively before the sun came over the rim of the prairie. The men fetched water from near-by springs and wood to start the breakfast fires. And soon the smell of bacon and johnnycake floated in the air.

The wagon train was very long and each wagon was assigned a place in line, but where the land was flat and dry, the billowing whitetops spread out far and wide over the landscape, each family going at its own pace.

At noon we stopped for dinner and to refresh the livestock at some convenient spring. White table-cloths were spread on the grass and, picnic style, the folks sat down to lunch.

The other ladies were very kind to Mrs. Reed. They dropped by to visit and keep her company so she wouldn't be so lonesome for Grandma. They brought samples of their cooking and exchanged reci-pes with her, and talked about the children.

In the afternoons, now and then, we saw herds of antelope on the horizon. So fleet they were and graceful as they skimmed over the ground that they seemed barely to touch it with their dainty feet.

"We'll be running into buffalo one of these days," Milt remarked to Patty as she rode on the box with him to get a better view.

On June 8, we reached the bluffs that overlooked the wide valley of the Platte River.

"We'll be traveling along the Platte River for many miles," Mr. Reed said, looking up from the map he was examining. "It will be much dryer than

the prairies we've crossed up to now. You'll have
good use for your sunbonnets and parasols, girls.
We'll be climbing toward the Western sun for sure."

Walking along the slow-moving river next day,
Patty and Leanna wondered about the little green
islands that dotted its surface.

"Do you suppose anyone lives on them?" Leanna
asked.

"Maybe they are enchanted," Patty answered.
"They are so green and pretty, and everything else
is so brown and ugly. Fairies could live on them."

"More likely Indians," Leanna said. "Father says
we are in the territory of the Pawnees now, and they
are much fiercer than those old Kansas Indians."

"I'm not afraid of Indians any more, are you?
They've gotten to be a lot tamer than they were when
Grandma was a girl." Patty's voice quivered as she
thought of Grandma and the stories she'd not hear
again.

"Did you see the Mackinaw boats on the river this
morning?" Leanna spoke up quickly.

"Oh, yes. We looked through Father's spyglass.
There were eight of them and they were loaded with
bales of furs. The men had to jump out and push
them over the sand bars."

"My brothers rode over to talk to the trappers,"
Leanna said. "They told Bill and Sol that there was
a big wagon train about a day ahead of us, and the
Pawnee Indians tried to break into their camp."

"Did anyone get scalped?" Patty wasn't so sure
now that she was no longer afraid of Indians.

About the seventeenth of June we crossed the South Fork of the Platte River

"No. Bill said the men scared them away with their guns. I heard Father say we'd have to double the guard on our camp tonight."

Just then Jimmy came running up. "Patty, Patty," he called, "Papa is going to take us to see the little dogs. Come on."

The boys, riding ahead, had discovered a prairie-dog village and they had turned back to take the younger children to see the odd little town built by these funny animals. Leanna rode with her brother Bill and Patty was mounted behind Puss, while Mr. Reed took the boys with him on Glaucus.

The prairie-dog village was a mile or two away, and as we approached it we could hear their shrill barking. When they caught sight of us they scampered into the little dirt mounds that were their homes, peering out timidly to watch us and causing the children to laugh delightedly at their innocent expressions.

"I want to get down and catch one for Mamma," Jimmy said to his father. He and some of the other youngsters tried, but none of them was quick enough to snare a little creature before it had popped into its hole. However, this adventure gave the boys something to talk about for days.

The next day we saw more trappers who were on their way back to the settlements with their Mackinaw boats loaded with buffalo skins. The river was so low that they could not proceed any farther by water, and they were anxious to buy horses and wagons to wheel their cargo to the settlements.

These trappers wore the hunting dress of the mountains, and the boys in our party looked enviously at their buckskin shirts with fringe at the bottom, and at their buckskin trousers and moccasins. I overheard Milt remark to Puss, "I'd sure admire to have an outfit like that."

The mountain men stayed in our camp that night, and bonfires blazed late while folks wrote letters for them to carry back to relatives. And accounts were sent to be published in the Springfield paper.

Mr. Reed bought some buffalo robes from them, giving them supplies in return. They needed flour, bacon, sugar, and coffee, they said. Some one sold them horses and they left next morning after consulting with our leaders about the trail ahead.

The valley of the Platte was broad, but the bluffs along the edge were steep and rugged, cut with deep gorges and ravines. Mr. Reed and some of the other men rode into them in search of game, and returned with a large elk they had shot. It was butchered and cooked over a hot campfire of buffalo chips—the dried droppings of the buffalo herds that roamed these prairies.

The next day Mr. Grayson and Governor Boggs crossed the river to hunt, and they shot the first buffalo.

We were traveling much faster these days. Mr. Reed seemed pleased at night when he could record in his book, "traveled twenty miles"—or sometimes "thirty."

"We'll celebrate the Fourth of July at Fort Laramie," he said.

About the seventeenth of June, as I remember, we crossed the South Fork of the Platte River. The country through which we had been passing was bare and desolate. We could see no trees or shrubs anywhere as far as eye could reach. Instead of the graceful wild flowers along the trail, there were cacti, some of which had flaming red and yellow blossoms. They were treacherous to the feet of the dogs and cattle, and the folks were constantly pulling the thorns out for the unhappy animals, and sometimes for the children.

The sun was hot, and Patty couldn't make up her mind whether it was more uncomfortable to walk in its burning rays alongside the wagons or to sit inside in the stifling heat. As we crossed the river, she and I sat in the dimness of the wagon watching Eliza churn the butter.

"It appears to me that this old river is rising rapidly. I guess we got here just in time," Eliza said as we rolled slowly down the slope and into the muddy water. .

On the other side, the landscape was as desertlike as before. As we rolled along through the dust, the dry, shrunken wagon wheels creaked, and sometimes down they sank almost to the hub in the loose sand. Winds drifted the sand across the empty plain, and faces and clothes were covered with gray dust. I almost envied the other dolls packed neatly away from it all. But then, if Patty could stand it, I could. After all, a wooden face can endure a great deal.

At a place called Ash Hollow, the trail passed a log cabin built by trappers who had had to winter

there the year before. Now it was being used as a sort
of post office by emigrants leaving or returning to the
settlements. Posted on its walls were notices of lost
cattle and horses and in a box inside were letters
addressed to folks back home, in hopes that those
returning East would carry them to the nearest post
office in the States.

Occasionally the bare monotony of the cliffs was
relieved by a few stunted cedars, and now and then
patches of blue lupin or gooseberries and wild cur-
rants were found growing near springs of water.
These springs became fewer and farther between and,
for the most part, the company had to drink the
water from the muddy Platte. The children complained about its disagreeable flavor. Pioneering was
becoming decidedly less pleasant, the farther west we
went.

Finally, one evening, there was a short refreshing
thunderstorm which washed the grass and laid the
dust as we camped near the bank of the river. When
it was over, a beautiful rainbow made a perfect arch
in the eastern sky.

"Red, yellow, and Irish green," said Patty to herself
as she looked out at it. But there she stopped, and
when I looked at her, her eyes were filled with tears.

The next morning the air was so clear that we saw
Chimney Rock forty miles away.

"What made it look like a chimney, Papa?" Patty
asked.

"Probably it is composed of soft rock and can't
stand up against the fierce storms of wind and rain

that are gradually wearing it away," he answered.

"Some day will they blow it all away and there won't be any more Chimney Rock?" Jimmy wanted to know.

"I suspect that might happen, Son," his father answered.

All day we traveled nearer to the queer-shaped rock. By late afternoon, dark masses of clouds began coming up in the west and soon streaks of lightning shot through them. The air was charged with electricity and Mr. Reed, standing outside the Palace Car, holding his pistol in his hand as he put on his oilskin coat, was surprised to see sparks of electricity rolling down the barrel and dropping to the ground.

"I'm afraid you will have a wet watch tonight," Patty's mother said to him. "Do you think you can keep a fire going?"

"Don't worry, Margaret. We'll make out all right. Every man has to take his turn at the watch, be it rain or fair weather."

It was rain that night, all right, for Mr. Reed and the men who stood watch with him. When he came back to the wagon at dawn, his clothes were dripping wet and he was shivering with cold. After a warm breakfast and dry clothes he was off again, however, and Puss was riding ahead with him. Nothing could dampen the spirits of Patty's energetic father.

The next landmark we passed was Scotts Bluff. Milt told us how it got its name. It was from a famous mountaineer trapper named Scott who got sick while his party was returning down the Platte

River to the settlements. His companions left him there to die, and the next year another party found his bones on the cliff. We didn't like this lonely place at all.

CHAPTER IX

FOURTH OF JULY AT FORT LARAMIE

EVERY DAY we watched great herds of buffalo come down to the river to drink. The plains were alive with them, and the crusty ground was rough with the imprints of their hoofs. Puss begged to go on the chase with her father and the boys and other men. Her mother did not approve. "It's too dangerous, darling," she said.

"But, Mother, Billy can always be counted on to follow close to Glaucus, and they are the swiftest horses in the party," she pleaded. "Besides, Papa says the buffalo will not attack unless they are wounded."

Her mother looked over at her father questioningly
and Mr. Reed nodded his head, so Puss had her way
and went on the chase. Patty and I watched her ride
off with the men, her cheeks glowing and her hair
flying, and we knew she was where she liked to be best
—at her father's side.

As Mr. Reed had said, we arrived at Fort Laramie
in time to celebrate the Fourth of July. Colonel
Russell's whole train was gathered there. Those who
were ahead of us on the trail waited until we arrived,
so that we could all take part in the festivities.

At sunrise, a salute of guns was fired, and the
youngsters jumped out of bed as excitedly as they did
back in the States on that patriotic holiday. They
all dressed up in their Sunday best and, after breakfast, paraded around camp and out to a grove of trees
close by, where a platform had been erected. There
they sang the "Star-Spangled Banner" and other patriotic songs, and the Declaration of Independence
was read. Colonel Russell delivered an address, saying that "here in the wilderness, almost seven hundred
miles from Independence, the last outpost of the
United States, we want to declare ourselves Americans
still, and hopeful of the future when all the broad
territory we have crossed will be gathered under the
banner of freedom, the Stars and Stripes."

Everyone clapped and cheered and then ran off
to the picnic dinner spread with the best of everything from all the good cooks of the party.

At noon the grownups stood up and, facing east,
drank a toast to those they had left behind.

"Our friends back in Illinois are toasting our luck at this very instant, as we agreed before we left," Patty's father said.

It was a gay and happy day—one of the last we were to have for a long, long time.

We emigrants were not the only ones celebrating at Fort Laramie, either. Hundreds of Sioux Indians were camped on the plains around us, and we learned from the men at the fort that they were preparing for a war dance. They were moving about excitedly, smeared with war paint and armed with hunting knives, tomahawks, bows and arrows. They were planning to fight the Crows or Blackfeet Indians, we learned.

We watched a procession of beautiful Indian girls dressed in fine white doeskin dresses, trimmed with bright beads. After them came a party of mounted warriors, two abreast, with green twigs between their teeth. These they tossed solemnly at us as they passed by, in pledge of friendship. How different they were from the poor Indians we had met earlier!

They were a deal too friendly, in fact, before we left their territory. After their procession was finished, some of the warriors came up to Mr. Reed as he sat on his gray mare, with Puss on Billy by his side, and motioned to him that they would like to trade for Billy and his rider. Mr. Reed smiled and shook his head, but they were persistent. They brought up buffalo robes and beautiful white buckskin costumes trimmed with beads, such as the Indian girls were wearing. Puss cast her eyes longingly at

After them came a party of mounted warriors, with green twigs between their teeth

these, but we were all quite certain that she would not part with Billy for all the beaded dresses and moccasins in the tribe. Finally they brought ponies, and even an old soldier's coat with brass buttons, thinking that to be the most valuable of all.

So determined were they to have Billy and Puss, that her father finally said, "We don't want any trouble, Puss. Perhaps you had better ride with your mother and the children while these Indians are about. We'll let one of the drivers take charge of Billy."

Puss did not like this, of course, and Mrs. Reed was becoming annoyed with the way they clustered about the Palace Car. They were curious about the stovepipe coming up from the roof, and some of them had caught a glimpse of the mirror opposite the door.

In order to see how far back their line extended, Puss picked up her father's spyglass and, pulling it out with a click, she trained it on the warrior host. This frightened them. They jumped back, wheeled their ponies, and scattered.

"They must have thought it was a rifle," Puss laughed. "I'll get even with them for making me ride in the wagon!" Every time the Indians came near to get a peep at themselves in their war paint and feathers, she clicked her spyglass at them and scared them away.

"I could fight the whole Sioux tribe with a spyglass, Mother," she said.

Finally they all rode off into the hills and we breathed a sigh of relief at being alone once more.

Apparently the men weren't so sure they would not
come back and, perhaps, try to steal what they were
so desirous of obtaining, and a heavy guard was set
around our camp for the next few nights. But we
saw the Sioux no more, and the only prowlers we
heard were the gray mountain wolves and the hoot
owls.

CHAPTER X

THE ROCKY MOUNTAINS

WESTWARD FROM Fort Laramie the oxen pulled the wagons over hills dark and shaggy with wild sage and cactus cruel to their feet. Along the way we saw the bleaching bones of cattle that had become too exhausted to go on, and when we heard the howl of the wolves and coyotes at night we realized that they were ready to pounce on any living straggler in this desolate wilderness.

The journey that had started out to be such a lark was becoming increasingly wearisome as we dragged along day by day beneath the broiling sun. Sitting by the campfire at night was not so pleasant as it used to be, either. Mosquitoes and buffalo gnats made the evenings unbearable, and everyone complained that their sting was much worse than that of the mosquitoes back on the prairies.

In addition, the grownups seemed to be worried about which road to take. The folks who were going to Oregon would turn off at the Greenwood Cutoff, Mr. Reed said. Those who headed for California had two choices—to go on with the Oregon people as far as Fort Hall and then turn south, or to take the new Hastings Cutoff that was described in Mr. Hastings' book that Uncle George Donner had brought with him. Uncle George read from it,

The most direct route, for the California emigrants, would be to leave the Oregon route about two hundred miles east from Fort Hall; thence bearing west southwest, to the Salt Lake; and thence continuing down to the bay of St. Francisco.

"This Hastings seems to know what he is talking about," Mr. Reed said. "I understand that he has guided several parties across safely."

"But not by that route, Mr. Reed," Mrs. Donner said. "George says that mountain man, Mr. Clyman, whom you met the other side of Fort Laramie, advised us not to take it."

"He did, ma'am," Patty's father answered. "But I know Jim Clyman. He's an ignorant sort. He was in the same regiment with me—Abe Lincoln was in it too—in the Black Hawk War a few years back. He came West after that and has been roaming around leading a rough life. Hastings, now, has had a good education. He is an Ohio lawyer, quite a young man, I believe, and enterprising. His book sounds as if he really knows what he's talking about."

"Mr. Reed's right, Tamsen," Uncle George said to his wife. "Clyman told us that Mr. Hastings was likely to be waiting up ahead at Fort Bridger to guide the emigrants across. He'd be a good man to tie to, if that's so."

"Three hundred miles is a big chunk to cut off, and that's what they say the Hastings Cutoff saves," his brother, Uncle Jake Donner, said.

Patty and I and the little Donner girls were sitting near their mothers, listening. Mrs. Donner didn't seem convinced, and she turned to Patty's mother and shook her head, saying that she thought we ought to stay on the well-known trail instead of trusting some man we didn't know, just because he had written a book. Patty's mother said she was sure that the men knew best, and it was very important to get across the mountains as soon as possible. Remembering Grandma's story about the folks who were caught in the snow and almost starved to death crossing the Cumberland Mountains back in Kentucky, my wooden head was inclined to agree with her.

We nooned a few days later near Independence Rock. Patty's father pointed it out to us on his map, and we rode over with him while he cut "J. F. Reed" on its surface, where were carved and painted so many other names of emigrants who had passed this way. It was on the north side of the Sweetwater River, along which we had been passing. Beyond it were the Sweetwater Mountains, rising abrupt and bare. The peaks were so high they touched the clouds,

Patty's mother said . . . it was important to get across the mountains as soon as possible.

and Patty asked if we would have to cross them.

"No, not the Sweetwater Mountains," her father told her. "But we shall have to cross the Rockies soon. There will be a pass, however. We have been climbing gradually ever since we left Fort Laramie."

On July 17, while we were toiling up these slopes toward the South Pass of the Rockies, as they called it, a horseman came riding to meet us. He handed around a letter addressed to "All California Emigrants now on the Road." Mr. Reed read it to the family, and he and the Donner folks seemed pleased at what it said. It urged them all to take the new route south of the Great Salt Lake, and promised that the writer himself would be waiting at Fort Bridger to guide them through. The signature at the bottom was that of Lansford W. Hastings.

Only twenty wagons continued to Fort Bridger, a hundred miles away. The rest turned off to Fort Hall on the road called the Greenwood Cutoff. Colonel Russell and Governor Boggs, Mr. and Mrs. Thornton, the Boones, and many others of the companions we had traveled with so far, left us here with "Good-by and good luck!" and a cheerful waving of handkerchiefs.

Besides all the people from Springfield, the Breens and several other families went our way. Uncle George Donner was elected captain of the little party.

The next evening, the eighteenth of July, we crossed the summit of the Rocky Mountains.

"This is the Continental Divide," Patty's father told us. as we stood on a rocky ledge near our camp and looked back over the ridge we had been climbing. "All of the rivers on this side run east toward the Atlantic, and all of the rivers on the west slope flow toward the Pacific. We have come a thousand miles from Springfield."

The snow-capped mountains rising around us were solemn and impressive, and everything was very still. In the west the sun was setting, and its light touched the rugged peaks with a strange, golden glow.

"Dolly, we are standing on top of the world," Patty whispered.

Our camp was near a stream called Pacific Spring. Mr. Reed pointed it out to us on his map and traced its course into the Green River, which empties into the great Colorado River of the West and flows down to the Gulf of California. Many wagon trains had camped here ahead of us, and the surrounding grass had been much fed down by their cattle.

The next day we crossed an arid plain covered with wild sage and dead bunch grass until we came to the Little Sandy River. Here there were thickets of willow trees and sufficient grass for the animals, and on our campgrounds the lupin was blossoming.

"It would be good to rest here a day or two, James," Patty's mother said. "Eliza has a heap of washing collected, and this is the first clear water we have seen for a long time."

"The rest of the folks seem to feel the same way, Margaret," he answered. "The animals are pretty tuckered out, and it won't hurt a bit to rest and fatten them up for a day or two. In a few more days we'll be at Fort Bridger, where we can do a little trading and get some blacksmithing done on the wagons."

While washing blossomed on the willow bushes, the younger children went wading in the cold, clear river and their big brothers went in for a swim. Everyone was in good spirits, for we were close to the end of our journey.

"Less than three hundred miles from California," they all said. "And Mr. Hastings is waiting at Fort Bridger to guide us there."

CHAPTER XI

FORT BRIDGER

BUT WHEN we arrived at Fort Bridger on July 28, Mr. Hastings wasn't there. He had gone on ahead with another party of emigrants, and the best he had done for us was to leave directions for following him.

"Mrs. Donner thinks we are placing a great deal of confidence in men we don't know," Patty's mother said to her father that night.

"But we must, Margaret," he replied. "It is late in the season, and to go around by the Fort Hall route would add another three hundred miles to the journey. These men could have no reason for deceiving us about the road ahead."

Mr. Bridger and his partner, Mr. Vasquez, the owners of the trading post, attempted to quiet any fears our people had about taking the Hastings Cutoff.

"Save three hundred and fifty miles, maybe four hundred," Mr. Bridger said, "No bad canyons and the trail mostly hard and level."

"What about Indians?" Uncle George Donner asked.

"None that will bother you. Only Diggers and Paiutes, and they're no account," Mr. Bridger said.

"What about grass and water?" Uncle Jake Donner wanted to know.

"Well, there's one dry drive—thirty, at most forty, miles. But you can cut enough grass at the springs to carry the oxen over, and fill your barrels with water. You'll make it."

For four days we halted at Bridger's Fort. The wagon tires needed resetting, and all sorts of minor repairs had to be made. Patty's father bought two more oxen to replace Bully and George who had drunk from a poison spring back on the trail and died. And, at last, Milt had his buckskin hunting suit. In fact, even Mr. Reed changed his dusty broadcloth for buckskin, and everyone purchased a pair of beaded moccasins from the Indians who had brought them in to the post.

One of the boys bought some Indian paint and fooled the rest into thinking he was Mr. Bridger's Indian son. Puss laughed about it as she told her mother, "He paid more dearly than he expected for his fun. He found that Indian paint isn't easy to get

And at last Milt had his buckskin hunting suit

off. He may look like an Indian for the rest of the trip."

On the last day of July we left Fort Bridger and followed the wheel marks where Mr. Hastings and his party had turned onto the new route.

CHAPTER XII

THE HASTINGS CUTOFF

IT WASN'T quite so smooth as Mr. Bridger had let on. There were narrow ravines and steep hillsides where the wagon wheels had to be locked to keep them from rolling down helter-skelter. The towering red cliffs on either side sent back the echoes of our rattling wheels, and the streams we crossed were red as if with blood. The grownups were worried, Patty and I could tell. Perhaps Mrs. Donner was right—they shouldn't have trusted a stranger to lead them over an unknown route. Mr. Hastings's book had not told of all these perils.

When we came out of the canyon of the red cliffs, we followed a stream which Mr. Reed said was the Red Fork of the Weber River. "It runs into the

Great Salt Lake," he said. "We'll be all right if we follow it."

"As long as the wheel tracks of Hastings' party show us the way, I reckon we can't get lost," Milt concluded.

But before we had gone very far along the Weber River, the wheel tracks led to a crossing, and there, stuck in the top of a bush, was a letter from Mr. Hastings. It said that the Weber canyon ahead was very dangerous. He was afraid that the party he was leading would not get through. Therefore, any wagons following should wait where they were and send a messenger ahead to overtake him, and he would return and guide them by a better route.

The folks all got out of their wagons and gathered on the river bank to decide what to do.

"Perhaps it would be best to turn back to Fort Bridger and go the old route that we're sure of," Captain Donner suggested.

"We don't dare, George," Patty's father spoke up. "It's already the sixth of August. Time is getting short to make it across the mountains before the snows."

Some of the other men mentioned that their provisions were running out, and they thought we should hurry along.

"What kind of a fellow is this Hastings, anyway? I thought he said he'd explored this route," Mr. Breen said.

A big man named Mr. McCutcheon spoke up. "The thing to do is to send on ahead and get this Hastings

Finally, on the evening of the fifth day, Mr. Reed returned

to come back, like he says, and show us a better
way. The rest of you camp here and I'll go on and
fetch him."

"I'll go with you," Patty's father said. A man
named Stanton offered to accompany them. They
packed food, sharpened their axes, and rode off down
the canyon. Puss wanted to go, too, but this was one
time her father was firm.

"Not this time, Daughter. We don't know what's
ahead," he told her.

For almost a week we camped at the Weber River
crossing. The delay worried everyone. Even the little
boys got impatient.

"Why doesn't Papa come back?" they kept repeating.

"He will, children, he will," their mother answered
each time, but she kept peering anxiously down the
canyon trail.

Finally, on the evening of the fifth day, Mr. Reed
returned. He looked battered and tired out, and it
wasn't Glaucus he was riding. Everyone gathered
around him to find out where the other men were.

"They are safe," he reassured them. "Their horses
gave out, and they had to stay with Hastings' party
to rest them. They'll be back in another day or two."

"But what of Hastings," they all asked. "Didn't
you bring him back to guide us?"

"No." Mr. Reed looked serious. "He refused to
come back all the way. He climbed with us to a high
peak and pointed out the route we should take.
It seems this Weber Canyon route he'd taken on

hearsay. He'd never really explored it himself. The route he pointed out over the mountain he had taken himself. He said there'd be lots of ax and spade work to do, but it would be safer for the wagons."

"Is this Weber Canyon impossible to get through, then?" Captain Donner asked. "The other train made it, didn't they?"

"Yes, it's much too narrow for the wheels to pass. We could see that. In some places they had to rig up windlasses and raise the wagons over the cliffs alongside the river. The rocks were so steep the oxen couldn't get a footing. One wagon, with its team, fell over a precipice and was lost."

The men shook their heads. Mr. Reed continued, "Their party was larger and stronger than ours. I'm afraid we'd never make it by the canyon route. The only alternative is the mountain trail. I followed that coming back. It's rough and we'll have to clear the brush, but we'll be more likely to get the wagons through."

For three days the men hacked away at the willow, aspen, and alder trees tangled with wild rose vines and serviceberries, following the trail Mr. Reed had blazed through the mountains. At night they came into camp with blistered hands and tired backs, and in the three days we were able to move only eight or nine miles.

The women sat around the wagons waiting and speculating on what lay ahead, while the children busied themselves picking berries in the woods. Some of the men were cross when they returned to camp, and Patty and I heard angry complaints that Mr. Reed had led us by the wrong path.

"It's harder work than they had counted on," Patty's father told the family. "Too many of the men can't do their share of it, and there are not enough of us."

This situation was helped a little the next day by the arrival of three more wagons which had followed us from Fort Bridger. They belonged to the Graves family, and their four men were a welcome addition to the weary road builders.

For six more days they hewed and hacked up the mountainside. The progress of the wagons was painfully slow over the boulders and big stumps. The families all walked. It was too dangerous to trust to the lurching wagons. One of our wagons tipped over on a steep sidehill, but the men got it righted again without any damage. The canvas tops were torn and sometimes almost pulled off by the overhanging branches.

Finally we reached the summit and could look out over the wide valley of the Great Salt Lake. Everyone was much happier. Perhaps the worst was over, they said. Only Mrs. McCutcheon was still worried. Her husband and Mr. Stanton hadn't returned yet, and everyone feared that they had gotten lost in the dense woods and missed the trail. A searching party had been sent out a few days before to try to find them, but they hadn't been heard from. Then, as we were rolling down the steep western slopes of the mountain, they all came up with us. Poor Mr.

McCutcheon and Mr. Stanton had been lost, all right. They were starving when the searching party found them, and they said that they had decided they would have to kill and eat their horses in order to stay alive.

Puss said to Patty, "Remember how afraid we were of Indians when we started out? I guess we're finding out that there are lots of things worse than Indians about pioneering."

CHAPTER XIII

THE VALLEY OF THE GREAT SALT LAKE

THE NEWS that Mr. Stanton and Mr. McCutcheon brought was not good, either. They said that there was still another mountain to cross before we came to the valley we saw in the distance.

When they heard this, some of the men grumbled angrily. They said very cross things about Mr. Hastings and his cutoff, and even accused Mr. Reed and Mr. Donner of being irresponsible, although it seemed to me that Patty's father had made the biggest effort of any of them, since it was he who had hunted out Mr. Hastings and brought back the information about the trail.

There was nothing for them to do but cut their way over another ugly mountain, felling timber, digging down hills, filling ravines, and rolling away boulders, so the wagons could pass. Doubling the ox teams, they pulled the wagons safely over a steep, sheer cliff, and finally we came out into the open expanse of the Salt Lake Valley.

Patty's father didn't look cheerful as he wrote in his little book that night, "Twenty-one days since we first camped by the Weber River—and we have come only thirty-six miles."

The next day we pushed on again, but this time it was easier going. The plain was flat and level, and before evening we were traveling once more in the tracks made by Hastings' party, so we knew that we were at last back on the trail.

Several days later, we camped at a strange place where there were twenty wells of cold, pure water, filled to the brim but not spilling over onto the hard dry ground around them. Little ones and big ones— they were all counted by the children, and one of the older boys let a rope down to see how deep one of them was. The seventy feet of rope disappeared without ever touching bottom.

The next day we crossed another dry, dusty plain covered with sagebrush, and came to another fine meadow with clear springs. Here a signboard had been set up, but the paper attached to it was torn in bits and scattered on the ground.

"It was surely a message from Mr. Hastings," Mrs. Donner said.

"I'm afraid we'll never know now what it said," her husband answered.

We were all standing around looking down at the tattered paper that we knew must have been a message of great importance to us.

"No doubt it's about the dry drive that lies ahead of us," Patty's father said. "It looks like birds must have pecked it to pieces."

Patty and Leanna began picking up some of the scraps, and Mrs. Donner, looking at several of the larger ones, said, "I think we might piece them together and make out the words."

Several other people started scratching among the grasses and sifting the loose soil through their fingers to gather the bits. Mrs. Donner laid the signboard on the hard ground and pieced out the puzzle, until finally she could read:

" 'Two days . . . and two nights' it says." More of the scraps were fitted in; then she read, " 'Hard driving . . . reach the next grass and water.' "

"Two days and two nights of hard driving to reach grass and water! It's a warning from Hastings, clear enough," Uncle George Donner said.

"That doesn't sound right," Patty's father spoke up. "They told us back at Fort Bridger that the dry drive was only thirty-five or forty miles at most. That's only two days' traveling. Two nights would make it twice as far."

"This Hastings is a scoundrel, I say," one of the men growled.

"Well, there's nothing to do but fill up our water

Patty and Leanna began picking up some of the scraps

casks, and cut as much grass as we can carry for the cattle," someone else added.

For thirty-six hours we camped by the springs while the men stored water and grass, and the women did up a lot of cooking to last out the trip across the desert, where there would be no fuel.

Then, beneath a blazing sun, we started across a dry, flat wasteland. About ten miles out, a range of rough hills loomed up.

"Will we have to cross them?" Patty's mother asked as she rode along beside her husband, each of them with one of the boys in front. Puss and Patty were doubling up on Billy.

"It surely looks as though we will," he answered. "Hastings' wagon tracks point straight at them. That's something else they forgot to mention to us about this dry drive—that there was a mountain to cross in the middle of it."

CHAPTER XIV

THE SALT DESERT

WE TOILED up the rough mountain range a thousand feet above the valley, and when we came to the top of the pass and looked out over the desert that lay ahead of us, even my wooden heart trembled at the sight. Under the noonday heat glittered a dazzling white desert—a desert of salt, they said.

"Good heavens, James," Uncle George Donner exclaimed to Mr. Reed, "anyone can see that stretch is more than forty miles."

We camped at the foot of the mountain that night, but there was no water to be had. The thirsty oxen were each given a quart from the shrinking supply that the men had stored back at the springs. As a great white moon rose to take the place of the burning sun, a chill wind cooled the hot atmosphere and, gloomy and shivering, the folks fell wearily into their beds.

Mrs. Reed hugged the little boys close as she tried to soothe their whimperings, and she told them everything would be all right. Even lively Puss seemed sober as she said to Patty, "It scares me to see Papa look so worried."

Patty answered, "It is so awfully lonely here." And her hand slipped under the pillow and clutched me to make sure that we two had each other still.

The two days and two nights passed and yet we did not come to the end of that awful desert. The water gave out completely and there was no more grass for the oxen. They dragged haltingly along in the hot September sun until they could go no farther. Some of them lay down and refused to move. The children cried for water and their mothers gave them lumps of sugar to cool their hot mouths. The wagons became separated, every family urging its cattle on as fast as possible.

Once, in the glimmering heat waves, we thought we saw a green, cool spot ahead.

"Water!" Milt called out, and tried to urge the oxen on faster.

As we watched, the vision of waving grass and trees receded, and Puss's voice cracked as she turned to her mother and said, "It's only a mirage."

The girls and their mother had been walking beside the drooping oxen, and Mr. Reed was leading Glaucus, reluctant to put any strain on the poor beast. Finally he said, "Margaret, I'm going to ride ahead and find water. Glaucus will make it and we've got to save the cattle. Our lives depend on theirs, and our wagons are too heavy for them to pull much farther. Most of the other folks are a long ways ahead of us."

He instructed the teamsters, Milt and Bayless, Walter Herron and Noah Smith, to keep the animals moving and, mounting Glaucus, he galloped away to the west.

The children and their mother trudged on. When Tommy and Jimmy got too tired to keep up, Milt hoisted them into the Palace Car.

In the close, hot cradle of Patty's pocket I felt as though my painted face was melting, and I wondered how my sister dolls were faring in their box in the wagon.

"Mother, my eyes burn so," Patty said.

"I know, darling. Close them and take my hand," her mother told her.

"Do you think the Donners have found water yet?" Puss asked.

"I hope so, Puss. If they have, we can't be too far off."

"Poor Billy! He looks thirstier than we do, and little Cash and the other dogs. Look how they are panting. I hope Papa gets back before night," Puss said.

The deep sand made walking difficult. I could tell that we weren't making much headway. The afternoon shadows lengthened across the desolate waste, and still Mr. Reed did not return. Eliza took out some of the corn bread she had baked before we started across the desert. The children munched it unhappily.

"It's so dry, Mommy," Jimmy complained. "Can't I have some milk?"

"The milk is all gone, Jimmy," his mother tried to explain. "Papa will come back soon with water. Eat the johnnycake like a good boy and I'll give you a lump of sugar to hold in your mouth."

Finally the darkness came and with it relief from the scorching heat. When the moon rose, white and still, Patty said, "How can it be so quiet? It feels as though we were at the end of nowhere."

"Nothing can live in this awful place—no birds, no animals, not even mosquitoes. Oh, why did we ever start for California! Springfield was so nice," Puss said bitterly.

"We didn't know it would be like this," her mother answered. "Mrs. Donner was right; we should never have left the old road."

Milt walked over to say that he and Smith had decided to unyoke the oxen and lead them ahead to water.

"They are ready to give out, Mrs. Reed. We're afraid they won't last till morning unless they get a drink. Walter and Bayless will stay here with you. If we're lucky, we'll meet Mr. Reed out a ways."

Patty's mother told him to do what he thought best. Then she and the children and Eliza climbed into the Palace Car and tried to sleep. No one said much. They seemed to have only one thought, "When will Papa come back?"

At dawn he arrived—with water—but with bad news also. It was still a long, long way across the desert. The other families were struggling to get there. Only the Eddys had finally reached the spring at the edge of the salt flats.

"I met Milt and Smith about ten o'clock. They were ten miles from water then. We'll wait here until they return," he said.

All the next day Mr. Reed impatiently scanned the horizon for signs of the teamsters and the oxen. They didn't come. At sundown he decided that the only thing to do was to pack as much food as they could carry, and the rest of the water, and start out on foot to overtake some of the other wagons.

After resting all day the family was anxious to go. Anything was better than this terrible waiting.

"Margaret, I never thought I'd bring you to such a pass as this," Patty's father said to his wife as they dragged along through the sand.

"I know, James," she answered. "If we had foreseen it, it wouldn't have happened. Now all we can do is be brave and hope for the best."

It wasn't long before the short legs of the little boys gave out in the deep sand. Their mother took one in her arms and their father the other, and they all walked on in the ghostly moonlight.

After a while I could tell that Patty was getting tired. She moved more and more slowly, stumbling often, and finally she fell to the ground. Puss helped her up, and she moaned, "Papa, I'm so tired. Can't we stop and rest a little?"

Her father spread down a blanket he was carrying, and gathered the family onto it. A cold wind was blowing and the shawls he covered them with were hardly enough to keep them warm. After suffering from the heat all day it seemed especially grim that they should have to suffer from the cold at night. Their mother and father tried to shelter them by sitting with their own backs to the wind and, calling the family dogs, Mr. Reed ordered them to lie down next to the children. Their warm bodies helped some, and soon they were asleep—the dogs, the children, and the parents, all huddled in one heap on the cold sands.

They slept for only a short time, however. Suddenly one of the dogs leaped up barking, and in a moment all of them had dashed off into the night as if to attack some danger. Patty's father pulled out his pistol as a large animal came charging through the darkness. The dogs headed it off, and Mr. Reed exclaimed, "I was sure it was one of our own oxen. The animal must have gone mad with thirst."

This frightened the children and they, too, jumped up and began to run. Their parents had difficulty calming them.

"Let's hurry on," Patty quavered, "I'm not tired any more."

For the rest of the night, we kept moving and, at last, about daylight we came up to the wagons of Uncle Jacob Donner. They told us we must wait there with them. It was too far to walk to water, and the men would be back with their oxen soon. Patty's father borrowed a horse and went on to see what had become of our teamsters and cattle, and all day we rested with the Donners.

In the evening the men returned with their oxen, and yoked them to the wagons and pulled us all to the spring. I shall never forget how the children dipped first their hands and then their faces into its cool wetness. Their mothers cautioned them not to drink too much at once, so they just knelt down there in the grass and touched it.

Our troubles were far from over, though. Only one ox and one cow belonging to the Reeds were there at the spring. Patty's father was out hunting the rest, and some of the men said they had all broken loose from our teamsters and stampeded away into the night before they got to water.

For several days we camped at the spring while the men searched for the cattle. Mr. Donner drove his teams back over the desert and brought our wagons in. And there they stood with no teams to pull them on. Other families had lost oxen, too—most of them lay dead of exhaustion on the salt desert. Some had disappeared into the night like the Reed cattle. There were Indians about, and not a few of the folks thought that these Indians knew more about what had become of the animals than we did.

Finally they gave up all hope of recovering them, and it was decided that we must move on. On the final evening before breaking camp, Patty's father sat on the step of the wagon, his head in his hands, looking more unhappy than we had ever seen him before.

"We started out with so much—more than enough to see us safely through—and now we have nothing. We'll have to abandon the wagons and divide our provisions among those who will give us passage in theirs," he said.

"We'll manage, James," his wife replied, her arm around his stooping shoulders. "On the other side of the mountains is California. We'll get there somehow."

The next morning all our provisions were transferred to other people's wagons. Patty's mother took out a change of clothes for each member of the family, and the rest was stored away in the Palace Car to be buried on the desert.

"But I can't leave my dolls out there for Indians to capture," Patty cried. "I'll carry them myself all the way to California."

"My child, you'll have all you can do to carry your own little self."

Patty cried brokenheartedly to think of her beautiful doll family buried out there in the sand.

"If everything goes well," her mother tried to console her, "we'll come back and get them."

Patty bent down to pick up a little glass doll dish and a play knife, and fork, and spoon that were lying on a trash heap next to the wagon. Just at that moment, I fell out of her pocket. I confess, I thought the end had come. I, too, would be buried in the dust of the desert. But I lay there only for an instant. Patty snatched me up quickly and hid me in the lining of her

But I lay there only for an instant. Patty snatched me up quickly and hid me in the lining of her waist.

waist, fearing, I suppose, that should her mother
know she had me, I, too, would be taken away from
her.

From then on I could not see what was going on.
I listened as hard as I could from beneath the folds
of Patty's waist where I was hidden, and pieced together snatches of conversation that would let me
know what was happening to my family. Once in a
while, when no one was about, Patty's hand came up
and pressed me to her heart as she whispered some
word of affection to let me know that she hadn't
forgotten I was there.

I gathered from remarks I heard that one of our
wagons still remained to us. Mr. Breen and Mr. Eddy
each lent us an ox and we traveled along with the
party in that way. The salt desert had been crossed,
and there seemed to be plenty of water now.

CHAPTER XV

ALONG THE MARY'S RIVER

ONE DAY all the voices sounded unusually happy because we had arrived at the Mary's River.

"We are on the main California trail, at last," Mr. Reed said.

"I wonder how long ago the folks we left at Fort Bridger passed this way," remarked Mrs. Donner. "Brother Jake and I think it might be well for us to move on ahead. Our oxen seem to be the strongest, and the grass is so scanty, it might be better for the animals to be spread out. We'd be glad to take your teamsters with us, Mr. Reed."

"Yes, you might as well," Patty's father replied. "I have no use for four men to drive one wagon. If they want to go with you, that's fine with us. Milt can stay."

The country we were crossing was rough, I could tell. Everyone seemed to be walking rather than riding, except for the littlest children. Evidently the wagons were heavy enough with the provisions that had been crowded in from the ones that had been abandoned. Sometimes the teams had to be doubled to draw them up the steepest hills. I could usually tell when this was going on by the snorting of the struggling oxen and the cross shouting of the men. As time went on they got more irritable with one another, and some of them were angry with the poor, weary beasts they were driving.

One day, October 5, as we all had cause to remember, there was a dreadful fuss as the drivers were trying to get the wagons over a particularly difficult hill. The team pulling our wagon got tangled with the oxen drawing one of Mr. Graves's wagons. Mr. Graves's teamster angrily struck the animals with his whip. Milt called to him to stop it, and Patty's father rushed up to straighten out the quarrel. Exactly what happened, I never rightly knew, although I heard it talked of a great deal in after years. Mr. Graves's driver must have turned his whip on Patty's father, and her mother, seeing this, ran up to interfere. The whip fell on poor Mrs. Reed and, at that, her husband drew his hunting knife and instantly plunged it into the teamster's shoulder.

"Oh, Papa, your head is bleeding," I heard Puss cry out. By this time Patty was sobbing hysterically, and there was a great confusion of voices, some angry and some sympathetic, as the folks seemed to separate into two groups.

"Never mind, Daughter," Mr. Reed answered her, "Here, look after your mother, while I see to this young man." But the Graves family angrily reproached him and told him to stay away. In a few minutes the man was dead.

Mrs. Reed was lying on the grass while Patty and Puss held damp cloths to her head. When their father came back to us, Puss exclaimed, "Papa, Papa, you must let me take care of your cuts."

"All right, Puss," he said quietly, and sat down. From the remarks that followed, I gathered that Puss washed and dressed the three wounds the whip had made on her father's head, and then they all huddled quietly together, stunned by the terrible thing that had happened.

Finally Mr. Eddy and Milt came over from the group that were consulting over the body of the dead man.

"They are completely unreasonable," Mr. Eddy said. "I certainly wish the Donners and the rest of your teamsters were here to force them to see sense. Their emotions are running away with them and they talk wildly of hanging you."

"None of them feels worse about it than I do," Patty's father answered sadly. "If my life will repay them for his, tell them to take it."

"No, no, James!" Patty's mother wailed, "You struck him in self-defense, and to defend me. You are not to blame."

"That's what we have been trying to make them see," Milt said. "Mr. Breen is still arguing with the Graves family and the other men. They don't know what they are doing."

Mr. Breen came over, at last, and reported, "They've agreed to banish you, Mr. Reed. You're to go on ahead, unarmed."

"But that's certain death, man. He can't get on alone and unarmed," Mr. Eddy exclaimed.

"They won't listen to reason," Mr. Breen answered. "I'd advise you to accept the verdict, Mr. Reed, unjust as it is, or they are apt to do you worse. If you can overtake the Donners, you'll be all right. They can't be far ahead."

"But what about my wife and children? Who will look after them?" Patty's father asked.

"James, you must go. Milt will stand by us," Patty's mother urged. "If you can get over to Sutter's Fort, you can bring back fresh animals and help. It's the only way."

That night, Patty and Puss and their mother wept bitterly, and the little boys cried, too, not because they understood what had happened but because they saw the others were so miserable. Mrs. Reed kept begging Mr. Reed to leave, for fear that something worse would happen to him.

Next morning, mounted on his gaunt horse, he slowly rode away. As I left I heard Milt whisper to

Next morning, mounted on his gaunt horse, he slowly rode away

Puss, "We'll ride out after dark and take his rifle to him."

Several days later we came up with the Donners. They told Mrs. Reed that her husband had camped overnight with them and that Walter Herron had gone on with him in the morning. This news made us all happy. At least he wasn't alone. The Indians would be less likely to attack two men than one. And when they got to Sutter's Fort surely help would be sent to us.

Our party was not free from persecution by the savages, however. On dark nights they crept close enough to camp to shoot arrows into the oxen. None of them was killed, but the poor beasts were already worn out from overwork and lack of good pasturage, and now wounds from the Indian arrows made them more miserable. Mr. Eddy's oxen had to be shot and, without his team, our wagon was of no more use to us.

There were left to us only two gaunt horses, one of them Puss's faithful little Billy. Tommy and Jimmy rode on these, while Patty and Puss, Eliza, and Mrs. Reed walked. Their few clothes and blankets were carried in Mr. Breen's wagon.

Eagerly they watched each day for the fresh ashes of their father's campfires and, when they saw goose-feathers scattered about, they knew he had meant them to see that he wasn't starving.

Traveling had become slow and painful. No one said very much as he straggled along. To make matters worse, another desertlike place had to be crossed which I heard them call the sink of the Mary's

River. It was only twenty miles—nothing like the awful salt desert, though the sand and alkali dust were deep and the horses floundered in it. The little boys cried for water, and Mrs. Donner gave them lumps of sugar to pacify them.

CHAPTER XVI

THE TRUCKEE

ALL DAY and all night we moved on, and as day-
break revealed a clear, pure river ahead, a hoarse shout
rose from parched throats.

"It's the Truckee River, folks," said Uncle George
Donner. "There'll be no more deserts to cross, and
we can count on sweet water and fresh air for the rest
of the way."

"Let's hope there'll be food, too," said Mr. Eddy,
as he cleaned his gun and set out to hunt fresh meat.

The wild geese he brought in were the first good food the folks had eaten for days.

Then, unexpectedly, help came. Mr. McCutcheon and Mr. Stanton, who had gone ahead to Sutter's Fort, returned with provisions, seven pack mules, and two Indian *vaqueros* who herded cattle for Captain Sutter. Luis and Salvador were their names, but they could speak only Spanish.

The best thing that Mr. McCutcheon and Mr. Stanton brought to the Reed family, however, was the happy news that they had seen Mr. Reed and he had made it to the Fort.

"He and Mr. Herron were so worn with fatigue and starvation that we didn't recognize them at first," Mr. Stanton told them. "For days they had had nothing to eat but wild onions and five beans, dropped from some emigrant wagon ahead. They stumbled into Hastings' camp while we were there. By this time, they are safe and sound at Sutter's Fort."

"Thank Heaven!" Patty's mother exclaimed.

"Mamma, it's the first time you have smiled since Papa left," Patty told her happily.

Mr. Stanton traveled with us from then on, and we no longer had to walk. One of Captain Sutter's mules carried our clothing and blankets, while Mrs. Reed and Tommy rode on another. Puss was mounted behind Mr. Stanton and Jimmy and Patty behind Luis and Salvador, the Indians.

"Wouldn't Grandma be surprised to see us riding with Indians?" Patty said to Puss.

"Mr. Stanton says they are Christians," Puss answered, "so they've got over their scalping ways."

Hidden inside Patty's blouse, as I was, I could only feel the Indian's hard back, as Patty clung to him. I wished very much that I could see him. I wondered if he wore paint and feathers like the Sioux, or whether he looked like the dirty, hungry Indians we saw back on the plains.

For several days we traveled through the valley of the Truckee River. There was plenty of sparkling, cool water, and grass for the animals. Mr. Stanton advised the folks to travel slowly and give the oxen a chance to gain strength for the hard pull across the Sierra Nevada.

Patty whispered to me, "We can see the mountains in the distance, Dolly. When we cross them we'll be in California."

It rained a little and the chill October air penetrated even to me.

"When it rains down here it snows in the mountains," Uncle George Donner said. "It seems to me we ought to hurry along without delay."

"Your oxen will never make it if you don't rest them, sir," Mr. Stanton said. "At Sutter's Fort the folks say the pass is never closed until the middle of November. Mr. Hastings got through last year in December."

"Well, you know best, I reckon," Uncle George answered.

We rested in the Truckee Meadows for five days and then pushed slowly on, crossing a low range of

The best thing . . . was the happy news that they had seen Mr. Reed . . .

mountains. In a steep, downward grade, an axle broke on the Donner's wagon and little Georgia and Eliza were tumbled out among the household goods. They seemed to be none the worse for the accident but it gave their folks a bad scare, and Uncle George cut his hand as he and Uncle Jacob repaired the broken axle. The rest of the party moved on ahead.

CHAPTER XVII

THE SIERRA NEVADA

As we traveled up toward Truckee Lake, snow began to fall. When the clouds lifted from the summits of the mountains and the folks saw that they were covered with white, I could tell that they were frightened.

"Oh, it will be awful if we are snowed in," Patty said to Puss.

"We won't be. Papa will be coming any day now to meet us," her sister answered confidently.

Along the edge of Truckee Lake the mules plodded through soft, deep snow.

"Why, there's a cabin," Patty called out. The

mule and Indian we were clinging to proved to be the best trail breakers, so we were somewhat ahead of the rest.

"It was built by a party that got marooned up here a few years ago, they told me," Mr. Stanton said. "We are close to the summit—only three miles or so."

We struggled on under a full moon, until the Indians made it known to Mr. Stanton that the snow had covered the trail and they were lost. We turned back and, arriving at the cabin we had passed, we found the Breen family already in possession.

However, they weren't much better off than the rest of us, crowded in the remaining wagons. Rain poured down in the night and leaked through the cabin roof of pine boughs just as it did through the tattered canvas of the wagon tops.

"The rain will melt the snow, won't it?" Patty's mother asked.

"It may not be rain up on the pass," Mr. Stanton answered in a worried tone. "When it rains lower down, it snows up above, they say."

He was right. Floundering through the drifts next day, we were able to advance only a mile or two before nightfall. Wet and cold from plunging into the deep snow, the folks gathered around a blazing log fire that night in frightened consultation.

"We'll have to abandon the wagons, there's no doubt of that," someone said. "If we strap our provisions to the backs of the oxen, we may be able to pack through."

"It will be slow going with all the children," someone else said. "Every grownup will have to carry a child. The snow's much too deep for the little ones to make it alone.

The next day they tried to carry out this plan. The oxen were not very co-operative. The children laughed to see them buck and try to throw off the packs by wallowing in the snow. But it was no laughing matter to the men who were trying to salvage enough food to get their families safely across the mountains.

It was late afternoon when we started, and Patty and I were in the lead, with Salvador and the donkey making a road for the struggling line of people behind us. In some places the snow was waist-deep and, carrying children and driving unruly oxen, they were able to move only at a snail's pace. Finally the snow got so deep that the mule we were clinging to kept falling head first into gullies filled with snow. Patty was taken off, and Mr. Stanton and the Indians tried to ride ahead and find the road, while the rest waited behind.

By the time they returned, the wet, discouraged families were huddled around a roaring campfire in a dead pine tree filled with pitch. The oxen had rubbed off their packs against trees, and everyone was too exhausted to struggle on.

Mr. Stanton tried to persuade them that they must. They could get through, he thought, if it didn't snow any more. But his words went unheeded. Weary men and women remained crouched by the fire, with their children bundled up in blankets and buffalo robes on the snow beside them.

Patty, Puss, and the boys slept in their strange, cold bed, with little Cash and their mother watching over them. The wind sighed in the pine trees and the snow fell softly. By morning they were buried under mounds of white, for a foot of new snow had fallen in the night.

Grimly we turned back. It was useless to go ahead. Near the abandoned cabin, the men built log houses, roofing them with branches, hides, and wagon canvasses. At least we should be protected from the weather, and there was plenty of firewood to keep us warm.

"Do you think Papa will find us here?" Jimmy kept asking.

"If we can't get over the pass, neither can Father," his mother was forced to tell him.

"Will we be snowed in till spring?" Patty wanted to know.

"We hope not, Patty," Mrs. Reed said. "We shan't have enough food to last till then."

The Donners hadn't yet come up with us. Finally, one day, Milt, coming in from hunting along the lake shore, told us that Uncle George and Uncle Jacob and their families, along with the teamsters, had built themselves huts on a creek that emptied into the lake.

"Uncle George's hand is bad," he said. "It got infected."

It was November 4 when we settled down in the cabins by the lake to wait until the snow should melt and we could cross the mountains. For more than a week it kept snowing, and then it stopped and the sun came out. On our campground the snow melted, and everyone looked forward happily to starting again on our journey.

Finally, on the twelfth of November, the Graves family and Mr. Eddy decided to attempt a crossing on foot. But it was useless. Before nightfall they were back, and I heard Mrs. Graves say that the snow was ten feet deep at the upper end of the lake.

More snow, and with it an air of gloom and despondency fell over the camp. The food was practically gone, and the men had to slaughter the sick, bony cattle one by one and dress the meat. Poor Mrs. Reed was hard put to feed her little family. Milt and Mr. Stanton roamed through the woods with their rifles, but the animals had all disappeared for the winter. They tried to fish in the icy waters of Truckee Lake, but the fish remained in its depths. For every ox she was able to buy from Mr. Breen or Mrs. Graves, Patty's mother had to promise to pay double when we got to California. And finally, they would sell her no more, saying, "I must think of my own family first."

For days at a time snowstorms howled through the pines, and it took all the strength the men could muster to gather firewood. Toward the end of November, Mr. Stanton decided that he and Captain Sutter's Indians could lead a party across the mountains. There had been ten days of clear and melting weather and, with the provisions running so low, several families decided to risk it. They were back before midnight the next night, however, and Mr. Stanton remarked, "We could see nothing but snow and the tops of the trees sticking out of it. The Indians got hopelessly lost."

For the rest of November the snow came down, soft and wet, burying the cabins almost completely. In another driving storm one night, the remaining cattle and Captain Sutter's mules strayed away and were never found. From then on, most of the folks had to live on the hides they had used to cover their shelters.

After singeing the hair from these, Mrs. Reed and Eliza cut them in pieces and boiled them for hours over the fire on the hearth. They dissolved into a vile-smelling, gluey substance that the children were forced to eat because they were so hungry.

On the long, dark days when the blizzards raged outside, the family sat by the fire and tried to think of stories to tell to help them forget their misery. Puss remembered all the tales about Daniel Boone and the Indians that Grandma used to relate. Tommy and Jimmy had never heard them before, and they sat quiet for hours, listening.

"Tell it again, just like you did yesterday," Jimmy would beg. And Puss would start in about the Wilderness Road and the homes in the clearings and the painted Indians who lurked in the brush when Grandma was a girl.

Sometimes they cried because their tummies ached from hunger, and their mother would give them cups of thin gruel made from the few remaining handfuls of corn meal which she hoarded.

They stayed in bed a great deal, with all their clothes on to keep warm and, lying there in the dim, smoky twilight, Patty whispered softly to me the thoughts that comforted her the most.

"Someday Papa will come riding over the mountain to find us," she said. "He'll have johnnycake and cookies for us, and he will never let us be hungry again. We'll have a house in California like the one we had in Springfield, with flowers in the garden and sunshine every day. Papa will send someone back to the desert to bring home my dolls, and Frances and Leanna will come over to play with us. Oh, Dolly, I'm so glad I have you to talk to. How dreadful it would have been if I had lost you that day on the desert!"

The days and nights crept slowly by until finally it was Christmas. How different it was from the merry Christmases of other years! Mrs. Reed had been planning for it, we found. She could not bear to think of her children going hungry on this day of all the year. Carefully she had hidden a cupful of dried beans, some rice, a few dried apples and a little bacon. They all went into a Christmas dinner. As the pot boiled on the fire, the children watched it excitedly, shouting as each stray bean or piece of bacon bobbed to the surface and made their mouths water in anticipation.

"We can pretend we are having turkey and dressing

and cranberry sauce, like we used to back in Springfield," Patty said.

"I wish we had the leavings from some of those
meals," Puss replied bitterly.

"Children, eat slowly; there is plenty for all," their
mother told them, as they commenced the meal.

A week or so after Christmas, I heard Milt and
Mrs. Reed and Eliza consulting in quiet tones one
night, after the children were asleep. It seemed that a
party had left on snowshoes a few weeks before and,
since they had not returned, everyone hoped they had
made it down to the Sacramento Valley, and that it
would be safe for others to follow them.

Mrs. Reed thought that she and Milt and Puss—
and Eliza, if she wanted to go—ought to try to get
through.

"I can't sit here and see my children starve. And
that's what they will surely do if help doesn't come,"
she said. "The Breens and the Graves will take care
of Patty and the boys if we leave what provisions
we have with them."

Milt seemed reluctant at first. "I'm afraid we'll
never make it, weak as we are," he said.

Eliza was willing, however, and she and Mrs. Reed
convinced Milt that it was the only thing they could
do with starvation facing them.

When Puss heard about their plans the next day,
she was eager to get started. But Patty wailed miser-
ably when she found out she was to be left behind.

"Be a brave little girl and watch after your
brothers," her mother told her, her own voice choking

I am going to bring you bread, my darlings

with tears. "I am going to bring you bread, my darlings."

"I'm afraid I'll never see you again if you go," Patty sobbed. "Please don't leave us, Mother."

Tommy and Jimmy cried and clung to her, too, and for a while I thought she would give in and remain with them. But she broke away at last, and Mrs. Breen took Patty and the boys in charge and tried to comfort them.

Four days and nights they were gone, and on the fifth day they came limping back to camp ahead of another storm. It was lucky that they did, for they would surely have perished in the blizzard that raged after them.

Poor Puss's feet had been frostbitten and Milt had carried her until he had dropped from exhaustion. The Breens took them in and cared for them, and I heard Mrs. Reed tell Mr. Breen they had crossed the summit before they had to turn back.

Patty was so glad to see her mother that she said she would rather be hungry than be left again.

We all stayed with the Breens after that, except for Eliza and Milt, who went over to the Graves's cabin. Poor Milt was done in after the struggle over the mountain, and Eliza came back in a few days to tell Mrs. Reed that they were afraid he was dying. Mrs. Reed and Puss went over to see what they could do for him, but it was too late. Milt was dead, and they buried him in the snow outside the cabin. We knew we had lost our most faithful friend.

"It's a death camp, that's what it is," Puss sobbed.

"Everyone is dying. Mrs. Eddy's baby died yesterday, and now Milt. We'll all of us just lie here till we die. I don't believe Papa ever got to Sutter's Fort. He would have come back to us by now if he had."

She was hysterical, and Mrs. Breen tried to comfort her.

"Here, darling, hold the light while Uncle Pat reads a prayer," Mrs. Breen said, handing her a burning pine splinter in hopes that having something to do would calm her woe.

"We hope with the assistance of Almighty God to be able to live to see the bare surface of the earth once more. O God of Mercy, grant it if it be Thy holy will. Amen," prayed Uncle Patrick as Puss knelt beside him holding the torch.

After that she was quiet. But as the days went by, Patty and Jimmy gave up trying to coax her to tell them stories. For she sat listless and still, only getting up to kneel beside Uncle Patrick when he prayed.

CHAPTER XVIII

RESCUE

ONE EVENING at sundown, about a week after Milt died, we heard a strange "halloo" ring through the frosty air.

"Glory be!" exclaimed Mrs. Breen, and hurried out through the door of the cabin. Before the rest could follow her, we heard her cry out in an excited voice, "Are you men from California, or do you come from heaven?" And we knew that help had come at last.

They were a party of seven men whom the people of California had sent up to rescue us. They told us how Mr. Reed and, after him, the folks who had made their way out before Christmas, had told of our plight and begged for help in rescuing us. There had

been a war in California and now it was no longer a
foreign country but one of the United States, and
that was part of the reason why they couldn't get help
to us. Patty's father had started out several times, but
flooded rivers and heavy snowstorms had forced him
back. But he was on his way again and, before long,
we should see him.

The food they brought gave the folks of the starved
camp new strength, and immediately many of them
wanted to leave for the valley. The men were worn
out themselves, and the trip wasn't easy, they said.
Three of them pushed on to the Donner's camp,
while the others rested in our cabins.

Six of the folks from Donner's, including Leanna,
came back with the three men. When Patty and
Leanna saw each other they both exclaimed in shocked
tones, "You are so white and skinny, I could hardly
recognize you!"

Twenty-three were to leave with this first relief
party. They told the others that help would reach
them shortly, too. All of the Reed family was chosen,
and for the first time in over a week Puss seemed
to notice what was going on. Everyone had to walk,
the men said. No one would be able to get through
if he had to carry a child.

Late on the morning of the twenty-second of
February we filed off through the pine trees, the men
with packs on their backs marching ahead to break
the trail. The older children kept up with them
pretty well, but the Reeds and Leanna Donner lagged
far behind, encouraging three-year-old Tommy to

keep going. Patty soon became exhausted herself, and when Mr. Glover, the leader of the rescue party, came back and told Mrs. Reed very gently that he was afraid Patty and Tommy would have to be taken back to camp, it was Mrs. Reed, not Patty this time, who refused to be parted from them.

"I can't let them go back. Those who are left there are too weak and demented to care for them. We'll all have to turn back if they do," she pleaded.

"I think you should go on, Mrs. Reed," Mr. Glover told her. "The other two children will make it, and what little food I have with me, I'll leave with Mrs. Breen to feed Patty and Tommy."

"But when will they be rescued?" Patty's mother begged.

"I'll turn back myself the minute we get to Bear Valley," Mr. Glover assured her.

Mrs. Reed was silent for a long while, weighing in her mind which course she should take. Finally she asked, "Are you a Mason, Mr. Glover?"

"Yes, ma'am," he answered.

"Do you promise me," she went on, "upon the word of a Mason that when you arrive at Bear River Valley you will return and bring out my children, if we do not, in the meantime, meet their father going for them?"

"I promise it, Mrs. Reed," he said.

Kissing her mother good-by, Patty said to her, "Well, Mother, if you never see me again, do the best you can." She seemed not to be crying. I guess she had become so used to disappointment that she

One afternoon the first of March . . . Patty sat on the roof of the cabin . . .

was learning to bear it quietly and, taking Tommy
by the hand, she turned back with Mr. Glover.

The Breens were not very happy to see Patty and
Tommy again, and would take them in only after
Mr. Glover had assured them that there was another
relief party on the way.

A week dragged by while the children waited. The
Breen cabin was very quiet with Puss and the older
boys gone. Mrs. Breen said to Patty, "I am missing
your mother, child, though it's lucky she is to be out
of this dirty hole."

"Soon we'll all be out, please God," said Uncle
Patrick, "though we're better off than many, for
we've lost none of our young ones."

The weather was warming up. Almost every afternoon the sun shone, and Patty helped Tommy up
the steep snow bank that buried the cabin, and the
two of them watched the sunbeams sparkle on the
snow. "Hurt, hurt," Tommy said and put his hands
over his eyes when the sun was too bright. After the
dim gloom of the cabin, the light must have seemed
strange to him.

One afternoon, the first of March, I have heard
them say, Patty sat on the roof of the cabin, her
feet dangling in the snow drift, as her eyes followed
the path of a flock of wild ducks in the sky.

"Birds are very lucky they can fly, Dolly," she
was saying to me. "Think how fast we should be in
California if we had wings. But only angels have
wings besides the birds. Milt and Grandma are with
the angels now, and lots of other people, big ones and

little ones who came on this journey with us." She must have looked down to earth again, for at that moment she sprang up with a cry, "Papa, Papa," and fell head first into the snow bank. Instantly her father had her in his arms, and she was laughing and crying all at the same time at the sight of him.

He told her he had met her mother and Puss and Jimmy, and now they were safe at Sutter's Fort in the valley.

"Where's Tommy?" he asked with a note of fear in his voice.

"Inside, sleeping," she told him, and led him down the hole in the snow and into the dark interior of the cabin.

Tommy did not recognize his father, and stared at him strangely.

"Papa? Papa?" he kept questioning Patty.

"Five months is a long time for a young one of three to be remembering," said Mrs. Breen.

"Of course it's Papa, Tommy," Patty told him as he clung to her, fearful that this stranger would separate them.

Mr. Reed had baked some sugar cakes before he left the valley, and he gave them to Patty to distribute among the other children in the cabin.

"Give them only one, and tell them to eat slowly," he warned. Then he went to the other cabins to give food and help to the rest of the sufferers. There were several men with him, and together they went down to the Donner huts.

They brought back three of the older Donner

children, leaving Frances, Georgia, and Eliza with
their mother and father.

"The Jacob Donners are too weak to attempt it,"
Mr. Reed told the Breens, "and Mrs. George Donner
refuses to leave her husband. He can't last long, poor
fellow. The infection in his hand has crept clear up
to his shoulder. It's dreadful."

Mrs. Graves and her children and the Breen family
left with us. We traveled very slowly—the children
were so weak. But everyone was cheerful. At last
the long wait was over, and we were to finish our
journey to California.

When we camped on the snow that first night out,
the men built a fire, and close to it they laid pine
boughs for the children to sleep on. Uncle Patrick
tuned up his fiddle, and for the first time in many
weeks we listened to songs and happy laughter.

By the next nightfall we had arrived at the foot of
the pass, and again we camped as on the night before,
and the strains of music floated out over the snowy
mountainside.

"Sleep well tonight, children," Mr. Reed said as
he tucked Patty and Tommy in buffalo robes by the
fireside. "Tomorrow we must scale the pass. There
will be no place to camp on the way up."

In the morning the folks noticed ominous clouds
gathering over the peaks, and wind from the south
was blowing hard. Three men were sent ahead to get
the supply of food that had been cached in a tree on
the way up, and the rest labored with all their
strength to cross the pass. Hiram Miller, who had

been one of our teamsters, carried Tommy, and Patty was bundled across her father's back.

We made the grade, and by afternoon camped in an open valley, among the pine trees. The wind kept blowing harder, and the men had to work constantly to keep the fire going. A storm was coming up, and by morning the driving snow was so blinding that all the folks could do was to huddle around the fire and protect themselves from its icy blast.

The food was gone, and Mr. Reed divided a small package of flour among the twenty people. The children's hunger was not satisfied by the teaspoon of flour, and the little ones cried dismally for more. The men worked heroically to keep the fire going and were exhausted by dark, yet they had to sleep in shifts.

Patty's father kept the first watch, but he must have fallen asleep because the fire died lower and lower and I could not hear him moving about to replenish it. I tried to cry aloud and wake someone, but what could I do? I was only a wooden doll! Even Patty could not hear my quiet voice. Finally the cold must have awakened the sleepers. Mr. Miller and Mr. McCutcheon sprang up and started to tend the fire. Children woke and began to wail, and Patty cried out, "Someone help Papa. He's so cold and still!"

The men dragged him to the fire and chafed his hands and feet, and at last I heard them say, "He's reviving. He'll come out of it."

By morning the wind was still blowing furiously, lashing the tall trees about so that the folks feared

they might come crashing down on us. By noon it
had quieted, however, and the driving snow let up.

"Those of us who can, must go on," Mr. Reed said.
"Another rescue party must surely be on the way,
and if the men we sent ahead are still alive, they'll
bring back food."

The Breens refused to go. They thought they'd
be better off to wait for help, and Mrs. Graves and
her children stayed, too. The rest of us pushed on
through the heavy snow. Mr. Miller again carried
Tommy, but Patty refused to allow her father to
be burdened with her.

"I can walk, Papa," she said. "You must save your
strength to take care of us."

Bravely she struggled through the drifts, but I
could tell she was getting weaker. Finally she stumbled
and fell and, as her father came to help her up, she
cried out happily, "Papa, I see the angels watching us.
They are out there among the stars."

"Reed, the child is dying," I heard Mr. McCutcheon
say, and my wooden heart turned cold with fear.

They wrapped her in a blanket and rubbed her
hands and feet as they had her father's the night
before. She was lying very still and I could no longer
feel her heart beat next to me. From the thumb of
his mitten her father drew a little piece of bread.

"I discovered it in a pocket yesterday and saved it
for an emergency," he said.

He warmed and moistened it in his own mouth
and pressed it between Patty's cold lips. Gradually
her heart beat stronger and she moved.

"I was dreaming of angels, Papa," she whispered feebly. "They were so beautiful."

"You mustn't see angels yet, darling," he said to her. "Remember, Mother is waiting for us down at Sutter's Fort." And Mr. McCutcheon said, "You are a brave little angel, child. You inspire us all to keep going. Now try hard to keep awake, and I'll help your father carry you."

Warmed by the heat from his body, Patty revived as her father carried her, and eventually we arrived at a place where food had been cached.

"Over the next ridge is the Bear Valley," he said. "There we will be safe at last."

Staggering through the snow, leaving a trail of blood from their swollen, frostbitten feet, the little band was met by Mr. Eddy and another relief party. They had horses with them and gratefully, though with only a few weak words, the three men and two children rode into the land of sunshine and flowers they had suffered so much to reach.

CHAPTER XIX

SUTTER'S FORT

SOFT, SPRING rain fell on us as we descended to the beautiful valley of the Sacramento, and we heard the songs of birds for the first time in many months. It was forty miles, they said, from Bear Valley to Sutter's Fort on the Sacramento, but it was the best forty miles of the whole long journey.

After the shower, the sun came out and a rainbow arched the western sky. "Grandma's rainbow," Patty whispered. "Dolly, it reaches from heaven down to Sutter's Fort, and there are Jimmy and Puss and Mother coming to meet us."

Beside a warm, dry fire in a neat bedroom, Patty's mother removed her dirty, ragged clothes, bathed her, and dressed her in fresh, clean ones. She was about to bundle up the old things and throw them away

"Please don't be angry with me, Mother, for bringing Dolly too," she said ...

when Patty reached out for the dress where I was hidden.

"Please don't be angry with me, Mother, for bringing Dolly, too," she said, as she drew me out into the light of day.

I could not see at first—it was so bright after the long darkness. But I heard her mother say, "Be angry, dearest! Of course not! I am only happy to think you had a little friend to comfort you through all those days of misery."

And so I stayed with Patty always. She could not bear to part with me after all we had shared together. We had been pioneers across the plains and mountains and deserts to California, and in that long year since we had left Springfield, we had known the worst suffering that pioneers can know. Mr. and Mrs. Reed and the four children soon recovered from their terrible ordeal and were healthy and happy once more. Many of the others were not so fortunate. The little Donner girls were orphans now, and many others had perished in those snowbound mountains.

Their tales were told so many times in the Reed household that I committed them to memory, and, should I be asked, I could recount them from beginning to end.

As the years went by in a beautiful land where there was never any snow, Patty and Puss and the boys grew up. Patty had a large family of her own and, at last, became a grandma just like the dear Grandma we had known so long ago.

She kept me carefully in a box of relics in her bureau drawer. A lock of Grandma's hair wrapped in lace, a little knife and fork and spoon, and the tiny glass dish she had picked up that day when I fell out of her pocket on the desert—these all lay beside me on her father's big mitten, the one which had concealed the crumbs that had saved her life. Now and then she opened the box and allowed her children, and then her grandchildren, to caress me with their soft fingers. I wished that they would take me with them out into the world again. But Patty would not let them. She told them gently, "She is very precious to me—my oldest friend. And someday she will be the sole survivor of the ill-fated Donner Party. Then she must go back to Sutter's Fort to tell the story of the children and their dolls who crossed the plains in '46."

EPILOGUE

After their rescue, John Reed took his family to San Jose, California. In 1856, Patty married Frank Lewis of Santa Cruz. Known as Martha Jane Lewis, she spent the rest of her life in that vicinity. Years after her death, her family donated her doll to Sutter's Fort.

ABOUT THE AUTHOR

Rachel Kelley Laurgaard wrote *Patty Reed's Doll* as a master's project at Sacramento State College (later California State University, Sacramento) where she also taught English. She later lived in Oakland for many years, where she died in 2000.

Read about other real-life pioneer children!

The Balloon Boy of San Francisco
by Dorothy Kupcha Leland

In 1853, San Francisco newsboy Ready Gates lives up to his nickname. He's ready for anything--whether it's shouting the latest headlines from a street corner, sneaking onto a river boat, or tracking down a missing gold miner. But when he crosses the bay to watch the ascension of the first hot-air balloon ever brought to California, his adventures suddenly take an unexpected turn. ISBN 978-0-9617357-9-1

Sallie Fox: The Story of a Pioneer Girl
by Dorothy Kupcha Leland

In 1858, 12-year-old Sallie Fox and her family leave Iowa by wagon train. They follow the Santa Fe Trail to New Mexico and then head west. Suddenly, Indians attack, stranding one hundred people in the searing summer heat. Sallie hovers near death. But, through grit, determination, and luck, she survives and eventually reaches California.
ISBN 978-0-9617357-6-0